THE
LONELIEST
GIRL
IN THE
UNIVERSE

LAUREN JAMES

HARPER TEEN
An Imprint of HarperCollinsPublishers

HarperTeen is an imprint of HarperCollins Publishers.

The Loneliest Girl in the Universe
Copyright © 2017 by Lauren James
All rights reserved. Printed in the United States of America.
No part of this book may be used or reproduced in any manner whatsoever
without written permission except in the case of brief quotations embodied
in critical articles and reviews. For information address HarperCollins
Children's Books, a division of HarperCollins Publishers, 195 Broadway,
New York, NY 10007.

www.epicreads.com

Library of Congress Control Number: 2017956218
ISBN 978-0-06-266025-1

Typography by David Curtis

18 19 20 21 22 PC/LSCH 10 9 8 7 6 5 4 3 2 1

First U.S. Edition, 2018

Originally published in Great Britain in 2017 by Walker Books Ltd.

For all the girls who've never felt brave enough to be the hero in an adventure story

THE
LONELIEST
GIRL
IN THE
UNIVERSE

Life is very much more exciting now than it used to be. You see I have something more to expect, to look forward to, to watch.

Charlotte Perkins Gilman, *The Yellow Wallpaper*

LIFTOFF FOR FIRST MANNED

INTERSTELLAR SHIP

06/26/2048 | CAPE CANAVERAL, FLORIDA, USA

Early yesterday morning, NASA successfully launched the first ever manned spacecraft destined to travel to a different star system.

The spacecraft, named *The Infinity*, is projected to reach the star system Alpha Centauri in less than fifty years, where it will enter orbit around Planet HT 3485 c. This exoplanet has a 99.999 percent probability of being habitable, making it the highest scored planet outside our solar system.

The Infinity is the result of billions of dollars of investment into solar sail technology. Space travel using this method of propulsion allows the craft to accelerate to the previously impossible velocity of 0.09 light-years.

Current calculations predict that *The Infinity* will reach Planet HT 3485 c in early 2092. Once in orbit around the planet, *The Infinity* will begin eighteen months of analysis to determine whether the planet's surface can safely support human life.

If Planet HT 3485 c is deemed unsuitable, *The Infinity* will continue onward to the nearest star system predicted to have an above 99.99 percent chance of habitability. The main mission of *The Infinity* is stated by NASA as being to "guarantee the long-term survival of the human race, by founding extraterrestrial communities outside of planet Earth."

The crew of *The Infinity* were chosen in a grueling decade-long application process that analyzed every aspect of their personal and genetic history. This screening process was followed by five years of intense NASA training.

The Infinity will officially pass out of our solar system at 22.54 EST tomorrow.

Check back for live minute-by-minute updates on the launch.

Click here to learn more about the crew of *The Infinity* or follow their journey via the official *The Infinity* social media accounts.

Don't forget to register to vote in the global referendum to name Planet HT 3485 c.

Read about the new commercial stasis service that is promising to help civilians live long enough to see *The Infinity* land on Planet HT 3485 c.

DAYS SINCE *THE INFINITY* LEFT EARTH:
6,817

I'm reading fanfiction in my pajamas when I hear a nightmarish sound: the emergency alarm. Pulling an oxygen mask out of the nearest wall panel, I sprint to the helm with my heart in my throat. There's a glowing red message on the screen, which reads:

ASTEROID COLLISION IMMINENT

AUTOMATIC TRAJECTORY ADJUSTMENT FAILED

ENGAGE MANUAL CONTROL

I'm abruptly filled with complete and utter fear. The guidance system has crashed. I need to take manual control, otherwise we're going to be hit by an asteroid within the next few minutes.

For what must be the millionth time, I wish that Dad was here to help. I try to calm down, taking slow, steady breaths as I tell myself that I'm brave and strong enough to do this—and even if that's not true, I have no choice but to do it anyway.

There's no time to panic, no time to do anything except *go*. My attention narrows. This is something I've practiced: I've been in simulations using force propulsion to minutely adjust the course of the ship since I could count. Dad trained me to operate the emergency program in case there was a problem that he couldn't take control of himself. He joked that if there was ever an emergency before seven a.m., I would have to deal with it because he wasn't giving up his lie-in.

I do exactly what I've practiced in the simulations, and use the joystick to line up the thrusters with the propulsion metrics on the screen.

The Infinity is traveling too fast to slow down much, but a minute adjustment of direction is all that's needed to make sure the asteroid misses us, if only by an arm's length. I check and agree to the trajectory angle calculated by the computer and initiate the adjustment.

I watch the screen, waiting. Outside the ship, precious fuel is being used to shoot nanoparticles into space. The force of the blast into the vacuum of space will turn the ship and change the trajectory—or at least, it's supposed to. I have no idea if it's working. If for some reason the propulsion thrusters don't work, or they respond too slowly, we could fly right into the asteroid.

I just have to hold on, and hope the ship can move in time.

Minutes pass.

Eventually, when I've long since started to brace myself for bad news or a horrific explosion, the alarm dies down and the screen clears.

COLLISION AVOIDED

I sigh in relief. By the time the asteroid nears *The Infinity*, our course will have been adjusted just enough that we narrowly pass each other.

I run to the nearest porthole to watch, hopping from foot to foot. It's coming too close—*impossibly* close. Glimmers of metal catch the light in the rough, uneven surface of the rock. Its shadow reaches me first, passing over the porthole and casting me into darkness as the asteroid approaches. For a second, I think that the computer must have calculated the angles wrong. It looks like the asteroid is flying directly at *The Infinity*. It's going to crash straight into the fragile hull of my ship, crushing everything in its path. It's going to destroy me. It's going to—

Every single muscle in my body tenses in panic, a tight knot spreading from my neck down my spine as I brace for the impact. I watch, wide-eyed, as the asteroid flies past the bulkhead in a graceful swoop.

There is no explosion, no crush of metal as the ship

disintegrates against the rock. Instead there's a wonderful silence as the side of the asteroid fills the porthole for two heartbeats. There's enough time for me to see craters in the dull brown rock, marks left from millions of years of impacts.

The breath leaves my lungs without me noticing. Then the asteroid is gone, disappearing in the wake of the ship, falling off into deep space once more.

I throw my head back and spin in a circle, overwhelmed with joy. I did it. I managed to control my worrying long enough to get the job done. I knew what to do and I did it!

It's only when the asteroid is a speck in the darkness, hidden among the bright stars, that I realize I've developed a raging headache.

By the time my headache is gone, it's midday—and I'm starving. I sit at the helm in my dressing gown and eat a lukewarm rehydrated chicken korma, reading through the ship's manuals. The close call with the asteroid has kick-started my anxiety. I worry endlessly about things going wrong. On some days, it's all I can think about. I'll lie frozen in my bunk, overwhelmed by the responsibility resting on my shoulders. I can't run this ship, not without Dad. Not on my own.

I need to be prepared for the next crisis. I have to know the ship inside out, from the boilers to the propulsion thrusters to the telecommunications and flight mapping. My schoolwork can wait—English literature is hardly going to be useful the next time there's a crisis.

By the time I reach page 97 of 14,875 in the manual, I'm losing focus.

As I scrape the last few grains of rice from my lunch into the organic waste disposal, I remember I haven't checked my messages yet.

I can't believe I've forgotten. Reading the new uplink of data from Earth is usually the first thing I do. Hearing from NASA is always the best part of my day—often it's the *only* part of my day.

I scroll through my inbox, skimming past the files of news articles until I reach the message from Molly.

From: NASA Earth   Sent: 06/20/2065
To: The Infinity   Received: 02/23/2067
Attachments: UC-podcast.zip [8 MB]; Worksheets.txt [20 KB]

Audio transcript: **Hi, Romy! Hope you're well, sweetie. Have you been finishing all your schoolwork? Your last message said you were struggling with some of the math. I hope you've sorted it out by now. I used to find math really hard when I was at school too! It'll all come together in the end.**

I'm sending you some more worksheets, in case you've completed the ones you've already got. By the time you read this, I think you'll be working on three-dimensional propulsion mechanics, so that's what the attached exercises focus on.

Let us know if there's anything you want us to send. I've also

attached a new episode of the podcast you like—it's funny. Enjoy!

Talk to you tomorrow.

Molly is my therapist and miscellaneous pillar of support. She was assigned to me by NASA after my parents died, to help me deal with their deaths—and my unexpected promotion to commander of *The Infinity*.

I receive messages from her every day, without fail, to make sure I don't get too lonely. Her first message was two hours long. I think I listened to it over a hundred times—maybe more. It was my constant soundtrack for months.

I've been alone on this spaceship since my parents died. The last time I hugged someone, smelled their shampoo, or even just spoke to them face-to-face was February 25, 2062. Five years ago. Right now I'm officially farther away from any other human being than anyone else has been since the evolution of the species.

I'm pretty sure I've forgotten what other people feel like. When I dream, I dream in screens. A line of text, a voice in my ear. Nothing real.

The things people take for granted, like seeing the sky, walking on soil, feeling the wind on your skin—well, I've never experienced any of that. I was born on *The Infinity*. I've only ever known its clean white walls; its sterilized atmosphere and artificial gravity; its gray floors, curving around the ship's hull.

I circle the same small space over and over every day, and

nothing changes and nothing is different.

I know I sound ungrateful to be here. But I didn't choose this life. Just because my parents were clever and multitalented enough to be picked to run *The Infinity* doesn't mean I'm anything special. I'm nothing like they were.

I should feel proud that my parents were chosen to run this mission. I should be proud to be the first human to land on a planet and create a new civilization. I get to carve out a new home for humanity among the stars.

But some days it's hard to remember the exciting parts. I get stuck in the memories. It's hard to focus on the future when the past is so distracting.

DAYS SINCE *THE INFINITY* LEFT EARTH:
6,818

The next morning, the computer sends me an alert:

HEALTH REMINDER

WITHIN THE NEXT 24 HOURS PLEASE COMPLETE:

40 MINUTES OF AEROBIC EXERCISE

10 REPETITIONS OF 8 KG WEIGHT EXERCISES

It's an exercise day.

I exercise on alternate days, and while it isn't the absolute worst thing in the world, I suppose, it's just . . . so *boring*. Mainly because of the endless running.

There's nothing to look at. I just circle the corridor around the entire circumference of the ship until I'm allowed to stop. At least while I lift weights I can watch my favorite TV show, *Loch & Ness*.

I stretch out my calves so they don't cramp, then begin to jog down the corridor. I could do this with my eyes closed.

The ship looks like a giant wheel, rotating as it flies through space. The centrifugal force of the rotation creates a feeling of gravity inside. The helm and the living quarters are around the outer rim, where you'd find the tire on a wheel. The stores are located in the center of the ship.

The only sign of the ship's rotation from the inside is the portholes. When you look through them, the stars spiral around themselves, over and over and over. It makes me dizzy to look at them, especially when I'm running.

I jog past the kitchen and the bathroom and the bedroom and the lounge area and the helm and dozens of other rooms, until eventually I find I've circled back to the kitchen. Then I do it again.

On good days, which don't come often, I love my ship and everything it represents. I thrill at the thought of seeing Earth II. There are going to be so many things there that have never been seen by human eyes before. I'll get to study the planet using priceless, brand-new equipment that's just waiting to be unpacked. I'll discover things that might change the fate of humanity forever.

The Infinity is the biggest, most expensive scientific mission in history. I get to be the very first person to see the results. I'm so lucky.

On bad days, I worry about my responsibilities until my gut

cramps and my head feels full of knives.

On my very worst days, I think of nothing but how vulnerable I am out here. I'm balanced on the edge of oblivion with only a fragile skin of metal separating me from the void of space. My only choice is to carry on into nothing, until the day that *The Infinity* reaches a new star system and glides into orbit around a rocky planet. If the planet turns out to be hostile—if there's scorching radiation from its two suns, or an atmosphere fierce enough to turn my lungs black—then I'll be lost.

I'd have to make the decision to keep going to the next hospitable planet, which might be many years' extra travel away. There'd be nothing to do but wait and hope that the ship reaches a safe haven before I starve to death. If I never find a habitable planet, I'll be trapped on this ship until the metal grows old enough to weaken and crack. The oxygen would be sucked from my delicate home; and when that finally happened, maybe it would be a relief, an end to the pointless existence of waiting for death from the day I was born.

Who thought it was a good idea? A life of never seeing a horizon or standing on solid ground?

This whole journey is a balancing act based on faith. We're all just hoping that *The Infinity* will eventually be able to reach somewhere safe. And for what? To satisfy the great human spirit of exploration?

My life is a gambling chip thrown carelessly across the universe in the hope it'll land somewhere my descendants can survive.

I represent the culmination of centuries of human achievement and exploration. But who cares if my name goes down in history, if no one remembers who I really am?

After forty minutes of circling the ship, I stop at the bathroom to have a shower. Then I check my inbox. I've been hoping that Molly will send me the latest novel from one of my favorite writers. Maybe today will be the day. An ebook arrived from Molly last week by another author I like, but it's set in space, so I don't really fancy it.

I used to read loads of science fiction, looking for characters like me, but it was all so *wrong* that it just made me feel more alone. Now I read a lot of romance novels. I like the simple ones, set on Earth. Stories that revolve around coffee-shop dates and walks in the countryside.

My fanfics are always set on Earth too. Museums and thunderstorms are so much more exciting than rocket ships and supernovas.

When I play Molly's new message, she sounds excited, in a way I've never heard before.

From: NASA Earth   Sent: 06/21/2065
To: The Infinity   Received: 02/24/2067

Audio transcript: **Romy, I have some big news for you today. We didn't want to tell you until it was all confirmed, in case something went wrong and we got your hopes up for nothing, but . . . I've had permission from the team here at NASA to tell you that a new spacecraft has just been launched from Earth!**

Ever since the tragic accident on board *The Infinity*, NASA has been building a second interstellar spacecraft to follow *The Infinity* to the new home of humanity on Earth II.

If we could have built and launched this ship any sooner, we would have. It's a huge regret to everyone involved that you've been alone for as long as you have.

As propulsion technology has significantly developed since your ship left Earth nineteen years ago, *The Eternity* can travel at much faster speeds. *The Eternity* launched successfully three days ago, and after a gravity assist around Jupiter it is now traveling at over 0.72 light-years, which is eight times faster than *The Infinity*.

Romy, by the time you get this message, *The Eternity* is calculated to be only one year away from *The Infinity*. Once in situ alongside your ship, the two ships will combine and continue together at the increased velocity of 0.72 light-years. You will arrive on Earth II on 07/15/71 as opposed to the original estimate of 04/02/92—a difference of over twenty years.

To be clear, *The Eternity* is a support for *The Infinity*. I don't want you to feel like you're being replaced. The spacecraft contains a significant gene bank for many species, elemental stocks for 3D technological printing, and a large supply of vacuum-packed food for use on-planet while agriculture is still being developed. However, your mission to establish a settlement on Earth II will still be orchestrated primarily using *The Infinity's* equipment and operating systems.

I know this is a huge change, and it might take time for you to come to terms with the news. I hope eventually you will be as excited about *The Eternity* as we are. Take today to process the idea, and tomorrow I'll send some exercises that will help you to work through your feelings in more detail. I want to make sure that you don't let this affect the excellent emotional progress you've been making recently.

What? *What?*

A new *what?*

A second ship is coming. Fast. I'm not—

I'm not going to be alone anymore? I'm going to have someone?

There's another ship coming in a *year!* I only need to wait twelve months.

I break out into giggles, leaning back in my seat and smiling at the ceiling. I'm not going to be on my own anymore.

And the ships will reach Earth II much more quickly! I've gained back years of my life—time that I thought was lost in transit. I'll only be—I count it out on my fingers—twenty . . . well, nearly twenty-one when we arrive on Earth II. I was supposed to be in my *forties!*

I can't believe it. I actually check to make sure I'm awake, because I'm sure I've had this dream before.

Another ship. It's the best news I could ever have imagined.

Who are they going to send? Who's coming?

I stare out of the helm window, straining my eyes against the infinite blackness, pressing my fingernails into my palms so hard they sting. I can't see anything except the silver pinprick stars.

How long until I'll be able to see *The Eternity*?

How long until it will be able to see me?

DAYS UNTIL *THE ETERNITY* ARRIVES:
365

The next day, when I listen to Molly's latest message, I brace myself for news that *The Eternity* has crashed, or that it was all a joke and there's not another ship at all; that it was some kind of test to see how I'd respond mentally.

I can't quite make myself believe it. Another ship. After all this time!

From: NASA Earth   Sent: 06/22/2065
To: The Infinity   Received: 02/25/2067
Attachment: The-Eternity-Mission-Outline.pdf [1.3 GB]

Audio transcript: **Hi, Romy. I really hope you're happy to hear about *The Eternity*, sweetie. The scientists here at NASA have been working tirelessly to ensure it's a successful mission, and to get the ship launched as fast as possible.**

I think that knowing you aren't so isolated will help you to

manage your anxiety. I know it's a lot to take in right now, so I'd like you to write a list of emotions that you felt when you heard the news. Everything you are going through is completely valid: anger, joy, fear—it's all normal and reasonable. If you want, send back a voice message telling me how you're feeling.

I've attached a full document with details of the mission and *The Eternity*'s timeline, so when you're ready, you can read up on everything about it.

I can't stop smiling long enough to eat my breakfast—a packet of beige goo that supposedly resembles porridge.

Will they send another couple like my parents? Or have they decided to send someone alone, since that went so disastrously wrong last time? They probably can't risk another pregnancy. One person is safer.

I let myself get caught up imagining they're sending me a handsome young man, but that seems too fantastical. Whoever it is, at least I won't be on my own anymore. I'm not going to be on my own *ever again*!

I'm going to have to share my space with someone else. That's going to be so strange. What if I hate it?

I feel restless, thoughts jumping back and forth until I can scarcely focus on anything but the new ship.

As a distraction, I decide to write a fic.

I know Molly wants me to write my bad feelings down properly in a diary, rather than writing fiction, but that would be too real. I'd rather escape into the world of *Loch & Ness*, where there's Jayden Ness—my favorite person, even if he's only fictional. There's kissing in fics too. *Lots* of kissing, in every Alternative Universe.

I always send my fics to Earth, but I don't think anyone reads them except Molly. Back when *The Infinity* was new, before I was born, there was a lot of excitement and curiosity about the launch of such a long-duration mission. Dad used to say that he and my mother were treated like celebrities, but it's been so long since we launched, everyone must have lost interest by now.

DAMSEL IN DISTRESS

by TheLoneliestGirl

Fandom: Loch & Ness (2042)

Relationship: Lyra Loch/Jayden Ness

Tags: Modern-day AU

Summary: Jayden is Lyra's knight in shining armor.

Author's note:

I had a bit of a catastrophe recently. An asteroid nearly hit the ship, but I managed to stop it at the last second. It was...stressful.

Anyway, here's what could have happened, instead of me trying to fix the problem on my own. Where's my handsome rescuer, please?

Lyra was texting when she first became aware of the shouting. She looked up to see a car swerving across the street, slipping on the wet tarmac. It was heading straight toward where she was walking.

She froze in her tracks, knowing she should dive out of the way, but unable to make her muscles react. The car was getting closer.

Suddenly there was a pair of strong arms around her, pushing her sideways, and she was falling just as the car skidded past them, colliding with a garden wall.

When Lyra realized that she was uninjured, she let out a breath, relieved and filled with adrenaline. She peered up at her savior, lying on top of her where they had fallen. It was her neighbor, the hot one from upstairs. He had brown eyes, sparkling golden in the early morning light. There was a quirk to his smile like he was trying to hide his amusement.

"You're OK," he said, his voice a low, calming murmur in her ear. "Relax."

Lyra sagged under his—very solid—chest.

"Thanks," she said, her voice cracking in an embarrassing way. "I'm Lyra."

"Jayden. It's great to meet you, neighbor," Jayden continued. "I just wish we were meeting in less exceptional circumstances!"

She'd never felt so relieved. The tension in her stomach, which had been building in a tight coil since she'd realized she was in danger, dissolved into nothing.

With Jayden, she was safe.

fin.

DAYS UNTIL *THE ETERNITY* ARRIVES:
364

My inbox doesn't contain any voice messages today. Instead, there's an MP4 file. A video.

I stare, too confused to open it. I can't think of a reason why Molly would send me a video clip instead of an audio message. NASA has always said that it's too expensive to send that much data.

Transmissions to and from Earth are sent by laser, encoded in binary. An antenna on Earth conveys the laser beams to *The Infinity*, where a light array picks up the signal and converts it back into letters, images, or sounds. The uplink from Earth takes a long time, and apparently video files just aren't feasible to send. It takes hours for the antennas to transmit them, compared with the minutes required for audio or text messages. What's changed now?

I've got a nervous tickle in my stomach at the thought of

seeing Molly's face. It'll be the first time I've seen a real human in years. I eye up the file while I eat breakfast, brush my hair, and get dressed.

I tell myself that I've got no reason to be worried. This is new and exciting. It isn't scary. That doesn't stop the itching concern at the back of my mind.

Eventually I sit down, take a deep breath, and click play. At first, the screen is black. Slowly it turns gray, and then white. Dark letters that I've seen more times than I can count appear.

Loch & Ness

As the familiar theme tune from the opening credits plays in the background, I double-check whether I've somehow opened a file from my hard drive instead of the message. But it's right.

NASA has sent me an episode of *Loch & Ness*. Why would they transmit an episode of a TV series to me—especially one they must know I've already got?

It takes me a stupid amount of time to realize why the first scene seems unfamiliar: it's a new episode.

Suddenly, I'm grinning. They've sent me a new episode of *Loch & Ness*! *A new episode!* Molly must have finally found an excuse to send it to me, like I requested years ago.

When I was ten, I asked Dad to ask NASA for more episodes, as I'd just finished the seventh series, which ends on this massive cliffhanger. The characters—two supernatural detectives called Lyra Loch and Jayden Ness—had just kissed for the first time. Unfortunately for me, *The Infinity* had launched before the eighth series aired, so it wasn't on the ship's hard drive.

In their reply, NASA said that they couldn't send me any new episodes because video files were too large to transmit across interstellar deep space. Instead they sent me a file full of *Loch & Ness* fanfic.

It's the single best present I've ever received, especially because it arrived just after my parents died. I read the entire archive, and then started writing my own.

I watch the new episode without taking my eyes off the screen for even a moment. Jayden Ness, the puppy-eyed and long-legged mixed-race selkie, and Lyra Loch, the no-nonsense feminist banshee, are trying to track down a fairy selling illegal love potions.

The new series must have been filmed a few years after the ones I've got, because Jayden looks a little older—his muscles are more filled out, and there are a few laughter lines around his mouth. He looks good.

I screenshot a few scenes, setting a picture of Jayden as my wallpaper. I replay his best lines, listening to the dialogue on repeat until I've memorized his latest witty one-liners.

By the time the credits roll, I'm giddy with happiness and excitement. I've already thought of three new fics based on this episode alone.

I'm about to watch it again when I notice the message origin. I shoot upright in my chair, reading it twice just to make sure. The video didn't come from Earth at all.

It came from *The Eternity*.

The new ship is talking to me. It sent me an episode of my favorite TV show. Why? Why would they bother using their transmitters for this? It must have taken hours to transmit. And why didn't they send me an actual message, even just to say hello?

I don't understand. My gratitude has dissolved into a mess of confusion and nerves. Someone on that ship knows I like *Loch & Ness*. They know that much about me, when I know nothing about them.

I should reply. I open up a message addressed to somewhere other than Earth for the first time ever.

I stare at the blinking cursor, trying to decide what to say. It hadn't even occurred to me that I might be able to talk to the crew of the other ship. I type **Thank you.**

I quickly delete that, and then feel like an idiot. This shouldn't be hard, but for some reason I feel shy. What if I say the wrong thing, and make a terrible first impression? Should I be formal and polite, or funny and relaxed? This would be so much easier if they'd sent me a message first. Then I could just copy their tone, instead of having to try and work out what to say myself.

* * *

From: The Infinity   Sent: 02/26/2067

To: The Eternity   Predicted date of receipt: 06/08/2067

Dear the crew of *The Eternity*,

I received your transmission today. *Loch & Ness* is my favorite show—thank you so much.

Congratulations on your successful voyage so far. I trust that everything is progressing safely with your journey to date.

This message is going to take almost four months to reach you, but I'm glad that we can communicate at all, regardless of the time delay.

It's nice to know that I'm not alone out here.

Commander Romy Silvers

I reread the message three times, finally deciding that while I definitely sound awkward, I don't sound as stupid as I could, so it'll have to do.

I send it off, then firmly tell myself not to think about them again. They're still closer to Earth than to me, so it'll take months for a reply to arrive. I should try to relax about it, at least for now.

I used to be able to have reasonable conversations with people back on Earth. The ship has been traveling away from the solar system at just under a tenth of the speed of light for my entire life, so even though light is the fastest thing in the universe, messages currently take over a year to travel through deep space between me and Earth—and the delay increases every day.

At this point, it's almost impossible to have a proper conversation with anyone on Earth. When Molly finally receives my messages, even if she replies immediately, it still takes another year (plus the extra distance I've traveled since I sent my message) for her reply to arrive. Though at least I get messages from her every day, even if they are out of date.

When I was little, messages would only take a few months to reach Earth from *The Infinity*. I was too impatient even then. At least as a kid I had Dad to talk to.

He used to send me letters when I got really annoyed with waiting for replies from Earth. Letters on actual paper (or rather, an old flattened food packet, which was as close as we could get), which he would hand to me over breakfast. It would always be something silly, like a formal invitation to play a game of hide-and-seek after lunch, complete with scrollwork, calligraphy, and a hand-drawn stamp.

Whenever I replied, it would never look as beautiful, however hard I tried.

I miss Dad.

I try not to think about my mother.

An hour after I've sent off my message, an email arrives from *The Eternity*. For a second, I think it's a reply, before realizing that's impossible. But they must have sent the message straight after the episode for it to be arriving now.

From: The Eternity   Sent: 06/26/2065
To: The Infinity   Received: 02/26/2067

Dear Commander Silvers,

I'm delighted to be opening up an official line of communication between *The Infinity* and *The Eternity*, since in relative terms we're now neighbors. As there's not an established protocol for how to enter into communications between the only two manned spaceships outside the solar system, I thought that an episode of *Loch & Ness* would be a welcome opening gambit.

I look forward to receiving a response from you in two years, which is how long it will take to receive a reply according to *The Eternity*'s computer.

I wish you a safe journey.

Yours sincerely,

Commander J Shoreditch (the guy on the other ship!)

It's a lovely email. It's a bit awkward and formal, but then so was my email to him. It's a thrill talking to someone new.

I'm rereading the message, trying to decide what to say in reply, when I remember that I already sent a reply to the episode of *Loch & Ness*, addressed to "the crew of *The Eternity*." I don't want Commander Shoreditch to think that I'm ignoring his email, or am too rude to talk to him directly.

I quickly access the transponder, trying to cancel the transmission before it sends—but it's too late. The message is already gone, shooting through deep space.

I need to send another email explaining, as soon as possible.

From: The Infinity   Sent: 02/26/2067
To: The Eternity   Predicted date of receipt: 06/08/2067

Dear Commander Shoreditch,

I apologize for my last message—I hadn't yet received your email when I sent it. It's very nice to e-meet you.

It's strange to think that by the time this message reaches your ship, you will only be a few months' travel away from mine. I hope that the two ships can unite and work together to make our journey as easy as possible.

I look forward to hearing more from you in the future.

Commander Romy Silvers

DAYS UNTIL *THE ETERNITY* ARRIVES:
363

Today Molly has sent me an email instead of her usual voice message, which catches me by surprise.

From: NASA Earth   Sent: 06/23/2065
To: The Infinity   Received: 02/27/2067

Hi, Romy,

We have some bad news for you. Recently NASA has been finding it difficult to gain enough access to the Deep Space Network telecommunications antennas to send you any large transmissions. Unfortunately, *The Infinity* has just been ruled a low-priority mission by the international board. This means that using the DSN to transmit high-memory data such as audio files is no longer considered a valuable use of space agency resources.

From now on, only email communication will be possible except in unavoidable circumstances—meaning that I'm not going

to be able to send you any more voice messages. Unfortunately, we also can't send any music or podcasts.

The Advisory Council thinks that this will only be a short-term issue, and it is likely that we may be able to resume our original broadcasting schedule in the future, once the political climate changes.

I'm sorry.

Molly

No more audio. The quiet happiness I've been carrying around since I found out about *The Eternity* drops away.

I had no idea this was possible. It's a scenario I've never even worried about—and I've worried about most things, realistic or not. The farther away *The Infinity* travels from Earth, the longer it takes for messages to arrive. I know that. I've accepted it. But to get no audio messages at all? It's all I have.

Why would my mission have been ruled as low priority all of a sudden? Have they decided that, since *The Eternity* has been launched, it isn't worth spending any more money on me?

Now that Commander Shoreditch is around—clever, competent, and NASA-trained—there's no point babysitting me anymore. I know that I'm the worst possible person to be responsible for an interstellar spacecraft. Even if NASA would never tell me that, it's the truth. They would never have actually chosen me to command this mission. They've only spent all this time looking after me because they had no other option.

NASA has always sent me *everything* I could possibly want to read: the latest scientific papers and newspaper articles; books; blogs; Twitter feeds; medical journals . . . I could read all day and never get through all the information that comes from Earth. I've tried.

Is that over now? Are they slowly cutting the ties between me and Earth completely?

What if I never hear Molly's voice ever again? What if I've lost her, along with the voices of everyone else on Earth?

I should have enough already; I know I should. My hard drive contains every TV show, book, and video game made in the twenty-first century, as well as thousands of songs, apps, and podcasts. I have nearly every YouTube video—and an entire archive of *Loch & Ness* fanfic. I have Commander Shoreditch now, too, I remind myself. At least he can still send me episodes of *Loch & Ness*.

That should be enough entertainment to occupy a human for an entire lifetime. Shouldn't it?

From: The Infinity   Sent: 02/27/2067
To: The Eternity   Predicted date of receipt: 06/09/2067

Dear Commander Shoreditch,
I got a worrying email from Earth today. Apparently there's something happening that means they can't send any audio files for a while. Did you get the same message? Do you know what's going on?

I guess there's no point in asking, seeing as you won't read this message for months. Hopefully it'll be fixed before you reply to this, anyway. I just needed to tell someone.

Commander Romy Silvers

I'm so jumpy for the rest of the day that I manage to catch my thumb with the scissors when I'm cutting the top off my lunch packet. Blood spills over the dried noodles inside, and I quickly wrap up the wound in my sleeve, pressing hard to stop the bleeding.

Get a grip, Romy.

I need to calm down. It's just voice messages. It's not that big a deal.

I use a first-aid kit to bandage the cut, even though it's already stopped bleeding.

Afterward, I eat my noodles, picking out the blood-covered ones as I take a walk through Google Earth.

I click down a street, not really thinking about anything, just absently taking in the trees and streetlamps and parked cars, frozen in time in the decades-old recording stored on my hard drive. It doesn't really make up for not being able to walk there myself, but sometimes, if I'm lucky, I can trick my brain into thinking I've actually been for a walk. On those nights, I'll dream of Earth and wake up happy, stretching out in my sheets, trying to grab on to the tendrils of my dream and keep them. Make them real.

There's a girl on the pavement, an old phone to her ear. As I click along the street, she turns and watches the camera as it passes. It's like she's staring right at me. She looks like a ghost, moving through the series of sequential photographs that tie together to make the Google Earth images. I click back and zoom in. She looks around my age—maybe fifteen or sixteen—with red hair, a long fringe, and bangles around one wrist.

I wonder what her name is; who she was talking to on the phone. I wonder if she remembers the day that a Google Earth car drove past and she turned to look, her picture caught in their records for all eternity. I wonder if she knows who I am.

I take a screenshot and leave her picture open on the screen while I tidy up. I stare at her, imagining the conversation we might have.

"Excuse me," I'd say. "Sorry, I know you're on the phone, but I was wondering if you knew the way to the cinema." I've always wanted to go to the cinema. It looks fun. Popcorn. Slush Puppies. "I'm Romy. What's your name?"

She doesn't answer.

DAYS UNTIL *THE ETERNITY* ARRIVES:
362

I'm feeling a little happier by the time my emails arrive the next day. It's no big deal, I decide. Sure, it was a shock at first, but I know that I can live without audio files. It was a nice bonus, but it isn't vital.

Then I read Molly's latest email—which is in text format again.

From: NASA Earth   Sent: 06/24/2065
To: The Infinity   Received: 02/28/2067

Romy,

I'm afraid that the situation with the Deep Space Network has worsened slightly. We will be completely out of communication with *The Infinity* for the next three days.

There's nothing to worry about at this stage—it will definitely not impact your mission. This is purely a political matter.

International disputes have unfortunately affected the control of the DSN antennas, but this should be resolved shortly.

I will keep you informed as to how things unfold when communications resume.

If all goes well, I will be able to catch up with you soon.

Molly

Molly's messages usually feel like a soft, steadying touch on my shoulder. This one feels like a punch.

I have no idea what the message means. What is Molly talking about? What is happening?

I try to keep track of Earth politics by reading the latest news reports, but it's so hard to understand what's going on between countries on a planet I've never been to. There's a cultural shorthand that I just don't understand, full of terms like "stock market futures" and "Electoral Colleges" and "FDA regulations." It's a foreign language with a whole vocabulary that I have no way of clarifying.

Besides, by the time it reaches me, the news is all out of date anyway.

I send off a quick reply asking for more information, but I know it's hopeless. It'll be ages before I get an answer.

I hope that whatever is happening on Earth doesn't last long. I need Molly.

From: The Eternity   Sent: 06/28/2065
To: The Infinity   Received: 02/28/2067

Dear Commander Silvers,

I apologize for getting back in touch so quickly. I had assumed that, outside of emergency scenarios, we wouldn't need to use the communications systems between ships regularly. However, today I received a message from NASA Earth saying that transmissions are stopping for a while.

I wonder whether the news raises the same warning bells for you as it does for me. It seems odd that transmissions would be cut off only a week after my ship has launched. What if something goes wrong with *The Eternity* while it settles into the voyage?

I haven't prepared for this in training. I admit that I may have skipped some of the more unlikely emergency procedures (I really don't think we're going to come under alien attack any time soon!) but I think I would have remembered anything that mentioned the possibility of cutoff data transmissions.

It's really ****ed up, if you'll excuse the language.

Regards,

Commander Shoreditch

PS I can't believe NASA has a line in their coding that censors swear words! Doesn't that go against the First Amendment? Can you swear in your transmissions?

Hi, Commander Shoreditch,

I got the message too. I agree, it's unsettling. I don't know what I'm going to do without my messages from Earth. It's never happened before. Did they give you any more information about why it's happening?

Oh, why am I even asking? You can't answer!

Romy Silvers

PS I don't think I've ever tried swearing in a message before, so here goes nothing. Shit. Ha! Looks like it's only you who's censored! NASA must have updated the telecommunications software after *The Infinity* was launched. Sorry.

PPS Do you think my dad had a habit of swearing in his messages? Was NASA so offended that they introduced censorship settings? That would be very funny. If so, I apologize on his behalf.

DAYS UNTIL *THE ETERNITY* ARRIVES:
361

I can't seem to do anything today. The news from Earth has thrown me so off balance that my chores seem pointless. I need to change my bedding, finish my schoolwork, check the status of the gene bank, separate my rubbish into different materials for recycling, and prune the plants in the sun room, as well as about thirty other things. But I don't want to.

I don't want to read anything, or practice my piano chords. I don't even want to rewatch any films on the hard drive.

I've seen nearly everything on the hard drive—except some of the more grown-up stuff, which I accidentally found when I was thirteen. I suppose it's unethical to send astronauts into space without some source of sexual outlet, but the videos just looked gross to me. Even the kissing, which I usually think looks lovely, was all wet and nasty looking. In fanfic it's always much nicer.

I don't know what to do with myself. I wrap my blanket around my shoulders, wandering through the living quarters and rearranging things at random.

I pick up a model of *The Infinity* that I made from food packets when I was four. It's one of the last times I can remember doing something fun with my mother, before everything went so badly wrong. The model is bumpy with spots of glue, the thick green paint peeling away from the plastic surface.

"The ship is a spinning circle, see, Romy?" my mother had said, while I applied homemade glitter and paint. "The spinning makes everything stay on the ground instead of floating in the air. Can you point out the engines?"

I push away the memory, annoyed at my brain for reminding me of her.

I move the model from a shelf in the kitchen to a low table in the lounge area, then decide it'll get in the way there and move it back.

I change my toothbrush to a new one, then remember I only replaced it last week. It would be a waste of resources to get rid of this one already.

I fluff up my pillows, tug the edges of the bedding straight, and pick a dead leaf off the basil plant on my bedside table. I put it in the kitchen bin, ignoring that it's overflowing already. Taking it to recycling just seems so much work right now.

Finally, I give up any attempt at productivity and sit on the floor of the lounge area. Legs dangling over the edge of the padded gray sofa set low into the floor, I eat three packets of dry cornflakes in a row, until my mouth is too parched to chew anymore.

I trace my fingers over the edge of the sofa, where the shaky letters of my name are carved. I don't remember doing it, but it must have been me.

On the underside of my bunk in my bedroom, where it folds into the wall, there are pen marks in permanent marker showing my height, with my age neatly written next to them in Dad's meticulous handwriting.

The last time he measured me, he shook his head sadly. When I asked him what was wrong, all panicked that I was getting shorter instead of taller, he said he was worried that soon I'd be taller than him; that then I'd be the one in charge of getting things down from the top shelves.

Dad showed me how to plot my height on a graph in my math lessons, making me work out how tall I would be when I was thirteen or sixteen or twenty, based on the graph's prediction.

The real measurements stop at age eleven, because after that Dad wasn't here to measure me anymore. I don't know if our predictions on the graph were right or not.

I wonder if Molly would be the kind of person to track my height, if she were here. I wonder what she's doing right now.

✳✳✳

That night I dream of Molly and Dad and my mother. All three of them hug me, their arms wrapped tightly around me. Their hair touches mine, and I can feel the heat of their skin, warm and comforting. I feel the tension in my muscles drop away. I'm so relieved they're here that tears well up in the corners of my eyes.

My mother is the first to leave. She strokes my cheek, and then turns and walks away. I call for her, reach out to try and grab her arm, but she ignores me. She tugs Dad, pulling him away from me before he can even say good-bye.

I bury my face in Molly's chest, heaving sobs that have turned cold and sharp and painful. I cling to her, and at first she holds me tight, humming calmly into my ear. Then the astronauts appear and start to surround us. I hold on tighter, but they tug her away from me.

I spin around, searching for Molly. I'm in a dark room, and there are eyes in the darkness. I can hear breathing. I can feel warmth on my skin as the astronauts slide past me.

I back away, bumping into something soft and sticky and slick. Everywhere I turn they are coming for me, pressing in closer until I'm surrounded by the stench of their rotting corpses.

I duck, trying to escape, but there are too many of them— hundreds and hundreds—burying me under their brittle limbs and— I'm alone in my bed. They're peering through the portholes at me. They stare like they want to know why

I couldn't save them; why I didn't help them; why I'm not good enough.

I wake up gasping for breath, shuddering in horror.

I thought I'd stopped dreaming about the astronauts. I thought the nightmares had ended years ago. I thought I was free.

DAYS UNTIL *THE ETERNITY* ARRIVES:
358

It's been four days and there still haven't been any emails from Molly. After dinner I access the detector's software to see if a message is being processed, but there's nothing. No laser transmissions have been detected from Earth for over ninety-six hours.

I've never seen it so quiet in my entire life.

I chew on the inside of my cheek, worrying at a loose piece of skin.

What is going to happen if the DSN antennas don't come back under NASA control? Is it possible that Molly might never be able to send me a message again—just because of politics?

I sit on my bunk, twisting my fringe between my fingers. I try to tell myself that Molly will be in touch tomorrow, that there's no need to panic. Whatever political disputes stopped Molly from sending me a message, they happened *more than a year and a half ago* on Earth! They will definitely be fixed by now.

It doesn't help.

I curl up in bed and watch *Loch & Ness* through half-closed eyes, trying to quell the feeling that something terrible is happening. I've got the half-real fear that creeps up on you in the middle of the night, making you think that there's a monster in your room. The kind that makes the hairs on the back of your neck stand up. But, unlike a monster, it doesn't go away when I pull the duvet over my head.

I'm being ridiculous, I know I am.

It's just one day. What does it matter if Molly doesn't talk to me for *one day* more than she promised? I can look after myself. I don't need her constant reassurance. I'm not a baby anymore; I'm a grown-up now.

DAYS UNTIL *THE ETERNITY* ARRIVES:
357

I sit and stare at my inbox, eyes glazing over until the screen turns into a blur of blank white space. I tug on the hairs on my arms, pulling them out of my skin one by one, focusing on the tiny sting as each one tears free. I blow on the hair littering the table, watching it scatter across the floor.

I wish I could punch something without setting off four dozen alarms and an evacuation protocol.

Eventually I decide to open up the flight simulator and practice landing the ship on the new planet to try and get rid of some nervous energy. The program is a 3D orbital gravity model built by NASA and based on the planetary mapping of Earth II. It simulates the ship's entry into the atmosphere and its descent and landing.

I run the simulation twice, bringing *The Infinity* down gently on a sandy alien hillock, plumes of orange dust curling up around the hull. A tiny simulated astronaut steps out onto the dusty planet, pushing a flag into the ground and raising both hands in the air triumphantly.

It's supposed to be me, but I can't imagine ever acting like that. More likely, I'd land the ship and then sleep for three days while I worked up the courage to even look out of a porthole.

The simulation is easy. Apparently it gets harder and harder, but I haven't put in enough hours to get to the advanced levels yet, when the flight simulator will expand into a planetary exploration system.

I'm happy to stick with this, for now. I really don't want to learn all the extra things I should be worrying about just yet—like growing crops in uncultured soil, or building houses, or raising farm animals. The thought of landing is more than enough.

Plus, the flying simulation really is fun.

DAYS UNTIL *THE ETERNITY* ARRIVES:
355

Today I decide I need to do something other than staring at my empty inbox in my pajamas, hair and stomach in knots. Molly always tells me that keeping busy is the best way to stop worrying. Instead, for the last few days I've been sitting around grinding my teeth in blind despair.

I need to push away some of my negative thoughts and just get on with my life.

I think I'm going to make jam.

First, I need to pick some strawberries from the sun room, which is part of the science labs. I don't really go in the labs much, unless the computer forces me to do some kind of check. But the sun room is my favorite exception.

It's not really a sun room—that's just what Dad used to call it, because when I was little I got confused about how photosynthesis and UV radiation worked, and why plants could grow in space.

It's actually just a lot of plants in a nutrient solution, sitting under an array of lights. The plants are an ongoing source of seeds to add to the seed bank, ready to grow in the newly created soil of Earth II.

Gardening is also officially endorsed by NASA as being good for astronauts' mental health—which I can confirm. Plants are easy and uncomplicated in a soothing, reassuring way. They just want light and air, and the containers do a lot of the work adjusting the water and nutrient and aeration levels. I get to enjoy the benefits without the pressure of something else relying on me for survival. The fresh produce is also a bonus.

I pick every ripe strawberry I can find, peeling apart frilly-edged leaves to find the juiciest ones hidden underneath the vines, and pinching away dead leaves to make sure all the plants have enough room to grow. My fingers are stained pink by the time I'm done.

I have to resist the urge to eat them all there and then. Instead I eat handfuls of sugar snap peas and radishes and runner beans. The tomatoes are almost turning red, so it shouldn't be long before I can make fresh tomato soup.

I think I'll change the light cycle of some containers from summer to autumn. I can harvest the broccoli. Maybe the Brussels sprouts. I'm trying to grow some bonsai trees, so they'll shed their leaves in the autumn cycle. I've always wanted to see crispy red leaves fall to the ground and try crunching them under my shoes.

Neither of my parents were really interested in gardening, so I took responsibility for the sun room as soon as I was old enough to understand how not to drown the plants. I loved the strange, waxy texture of the leaves, and how plants could be so fragile and strong all at once. It's difficult to imagine the precious organisms spreading across an entire planet without anyone to take care of them. Somehow they survive on mountains and in deserts and underwater without any defenses.

I take my harvest back to the kitchen and microwave the strawberries until they're soft and hot, then pour in a whole bag of sugar. I can only find a dessert spoon to stir the mixture with, so I have to keep dropping it when my fingers get too close to the jam and start to burn. The smell of the molten fruit gives me hiccups.

I microwave the mixture again, bending over to look through the window at the rolling red liquid. My mouth starts watering, just imagining the taste. I try to ignore the hiccups, which won't go away.

It's only when the jam is ready that I realize I don't have any jars. I pour the hot liquid into my mugs, lining them up on the worktop, and cut circles out of old food cartons to press down into the surface of each. I'll probably eat it pretty quickly, anyway. I can drink from a bowl until then.

I lie upside down on the sofa and gulp down water, pinching my nose, but the hiccups persevere.

Unable to resist, I eat four spoonfuls of jam straight from the mug. It's so hot that I scald my tongue, in a way that means I won't be able to taste anything for days. It gets rid of the hiccups, though.

And finally, *finally*, I feel a little better. I can do this. I can survive alone until Molly finds a way to speak to me again. I believe in her. It won't be long. She won't give up until she's fought everyone who tries to stand between us. She's going to come back to me.

DAYS UNTIL *THE ETERNITY* ARRIVES:
354

When I check my inbox for messages, it's still empty.

Determined to ignore it, I force myself to do some studying. When Dad was alive, we used to spend hours training while he taught me everything that an astronaut could possibly need to know. I was getting quite good, for an eleven-year-old.

Back then it didn't matter that I didn't know everything, because if there had been an emergency, Dad would have dealt with it. If it was a good day, my mother might have helped too.

Now that it really does matter, I find it harder to focus. I pull up some astrophysics problems and read the first question.

A twin leaves Earth on a spaceship of mass 3×10^2 kg, which is traveling at a speed that an Earth-based observer measures to be +0.600c. After the spaceship has been traveling for 8 light-years, the second twin departs Earth in a faster spaceship traveling at a speed of +0.750c, as measured by an Earth-based observer.

According to the theory of special relativity, what is the difference between their ages when they arrive at a planet 27 light-years away from Earth?

Immediately I know what I'm supposed to do. I can barely write fast enough to keep up with my brain, scribbling down time dilation equations and drawing diagrams of the forces, masses, and accelerations involved.

I get swept up in the joy of stretching myself, of being able to *feel* just how clever my brain can be sometimes. When I look at a problem and immediately know what to do, it feels like I'm flying. Sometimes I have dreams about doing math, just because that feeling is so wonderful.

But then, as always, I start criticizing myself. A voice in my head tells me that I don't know what I'm doing, that nothing I've written is right. I start panicking that really I'm not clever at all. I know, deep down, that if there was ever an actual emergency where I needed to use this stuff, my mind would go blank. I wouldn't be able to do it. My brain would jam, clogged up with that imaginary pressure and fear.

It's been like this ever since Dad died. I just . . . stopped studying. I couldn't—and wouldn't—learn this stuff without him. When NASA found out, Molly was put on my case to restart my training.

It's amazing how quickly the advanced astrophysics dropped out of my mind. I'm learning things now that I used to know—things that Dad made sound so easy to eleven-year-old Romy. But now, I'm always finding fault with myself. I usually just look up the answer at the end of the textbook. It's frustrating.

I'm erasing my failed calculations when a notification in the corner of the screen catches my eye. My heart skips a beat. A message is coming in.

I open the program for the detector, unable to resist watching the data packet arrive at the transponder. I need to know. Is it from *The Eternity* or Earth? Please, please, *please* let it be Earth. Let it be Molly.

The message trickles in, fragments at a time.

From: NASA Earth   Sent: 07/02/2065
To: The Infinity   Received: 03/08/2067

TRANS [Message incomplete]

I jiggle my knee, wishing I could hurry it up.

TRANSMISSIONS [Message incomplete]

I should go and do something while I wait, instead of sitting here watching it, but the scared feeling won't go away.

Something important is happening, and I can't make myself look away from the screen.

TRANSMISSIONS POSTPONED. WA [Message incomplete]

Transmissions postponed? *Again?*

R ON EARTH. [Message incomplete]

War on Earth. There's a war happening on Earth? I wait for more, but that's it. That's the whole message.

From: NASA Earth   Sent: 07/02/2065
To: The Infinity   Received: 03/08/2067

TRANSMISSIONS POSTPONED. WAR ON EARTH.
MOLLY

How could a war stop her from communicating with me? I wrap my arms around my chest, gnawing at a sore spot on the inside of my cheek where I've torn the skin from chewing at it. It would heal up if I left it alone, but I know I won't. I'll prod and rub at it until it's sore and inflamed.

Molly said that international disputes meant that NASA wasn't allowed to use the DSN antennas to communicate with me. If a full-scale war has broken out, it must be stopping NASA from accessing the antennas at all.

I'm itching for more information, desperate to know just what is happening on Earth. What kind of war is it? Will there be actual fighting, or is this just a political stalemate?

I sit at the helm for hours, staring at the detector and hoping to see even a single letter more. But there's nothing. War has started on Earth, and I've been cut off.

What do I do next?

I fetch my teddy from my bunk and snuggle my face into his fur, breathing in his familiar scent. My mother made him for me out of an old pillowcase before I was born, to keep her hands busy while Dad was working.

My conception was a surprise (or as Dad used to say, a "happy accident"). NASA hadn't planned for any children to be born until the ship arrived at Earth II, so there was twenty years' worth of food piled on top of the childcare supplies in the stores.

To make sure that I had a crib to sleep in and diapers to wear, Dad had to sift through the endless towers of supplies in the ship's center. Apparently, my mother kept trying to help. He had to make her stop, in case she hurt herself. Instead, while Dad excavated the depths of the stores, she spent hours sewing me a teddy bear. The fur's starting to unravel now, but I still love it.

However much I hate to think about her, I can't bear to give up my teddy. He's a reminder of the happier times during my childhood. So I keep him, despite everything.

I'm still staring into space when another message arrives, this time from *The Eternity*. For the transmissions to arrive so close together, Commander Shoreditch must have written it as soon as he read the message from Earth. Despite my worrying, I note how nice it is of him to think of me like that.

From: The Eternity   Sent: 07/30/2065
To: The Infinity   Received: 03/08/2067

Commander Silvers,

I just heard the news from NASA. I'm not going to lie, I'm more than a little worried. Before I left Earth there were a number of ongoing political tensions, and I knew war was a possibility, but somehow I still never expected it—or thought that it might affect my mission.

I can't really process what's happening. It's like the world has become a completely different place already, only a month after I left.

I hope you're OK, Commander Silvers. This is a big thing—it's perfectly natural if you're a bit unnerved. I'm here if you need to talk. I know how much it can help to speak to someone, even if you know there's no reply coming anytime soon.

Commander Shoreditch

I'm so tired of being abandoned. Commander Shoreditch's message is reassuring, but it hasn't helped. I'm exhausted, in every way.

Losing Molly is bringing back the awful feeling of when I lost my parents—less severe, but exactly the same. It's this horrible drop in my stomach, like when the artificial gravity malfunctions and everything stumbles, tilting sideways momentarily.

Love takes so much energy, and it just leads to pain. I think it's probably best for people to be self-sufficient. If I was strong enough to be independent, then I wouldn't be so desperately lonely, I'm sure of it.

I just want someone who *holds on*. Someone who won't ever let me go, whatever tries to tear us apart. Is that too much to ask?

I'LL HOLD YOU

by TheLoneliestGirl

Fandom: Loch & Ness (2042)
Relationship: Lyra Loch/Jayden Ness
Tags: Hurt/comfort, canon-compliant
Summary: Lyra gets hurt in the field.

Author's Note:

I'm not sure why I'm sending this anymore, when I know Molly won't be able to read it.

"Jayden," Lyra cried, grabbing on to his arm. "It hurts."

Tears ran down her cheeks, mixing with the rain.

Jayden's hands were pressed against her stomach, trying to quench the flow of blood from the werewolf bite. She could see it trickling between his fingers, staining his skin a red so dark it was almost black.

"Lyra! Don't you give up on me, Lyra, not yet. I need you. Just hold on a little longer," he said, pressing his forehead to hers. It was a circle of heat in the cold numbness spreading through her. "Lyra, I've got you. The ambulance is on its way."

"I can't . . . ," she gasped.

"You can, Lyra," he said fiercely. Teardrops clung to the tips of his long eyelashes. "You can do anything. You're stronger than you realize. I believe in you, Lyra Loch."

"We never even . . . ," she said, thinking of all the missed opportunities, the almosts. They'd never even kissed, and now she was going to die.

57

"We will," he said, and she could feel his breath, soft against her cheek. "We will. This isn't the end."

Then she heard the sirens, and summoned up all her strength. "We will," she repeated.

fin.

DAYS UNTIL *THE ETERNITY* ARRIVES:
346

From: The Infinity

To: The Eternity

Sent: 03/16/2067

Predicted date of receipt: 06/20/2067

Hi, Commander Shoreditch,

I hope all is well on *The Eternity*. I'm writing because I've been going through all the news articles that NASA has sent me over the last three years, looking for information about Earth's political climate and cursing myself for not reading about it more thoroughly in the first place.

There's been the usual political tension between countries for months, but nothing that I would expect to become a full-blown war this quickly.

Besides which, how could a war even have affected the DSN facilities that NASA uses to communicate with our ships? The telecommunication antennas are located in countries with very strong alliances—the United States, Spain, and Australia. For them to suddenly engage in war doesn't seem feasible. Not as I currently understand it. At the very least, NASA would still have access to the antenna in California. They should be able to send short messages regularly as the Earth rotates and points the antenna in our direction.

In the past, NASA has filtered the information they transmit to me, leaving gaps in newspaper articles. I think they censor out any media content with a personal connection to me and *The Infinity* so I don't get upset.

It makes sense that they'd do the same for news about the war. I think they were trying to stop me from panicking.

You have more recent knowledge of Earth's political situation. Please tell me everything that you know, even if your response won't reach me for months. I can't work out how the jigsaw pieces fit together in a way that explains this situation.

Romy Silvers

I wonder where Molly is now. I think I'm going to carry on sending her messages every day, along with any fics I write, just in case there's a chance she's reading them. She'd be worried about me if I stopped.

I just wish I knew if she's still there. I hope Molly is waiting in the lab for permission to send me messages once the war has died down.

What has she been doing while her last message traveled through space toward me?

Is she dead?

DAYS UNTIL *THE ETERNITY* ARRIVES:
338

I think I've worked out a way to contact Molly. I need to get in touch with someone on Earth besides NASA. Even if they've stopped using their antennas because of the war, there must be someone else picking up signals, on some continent, in some other organization. If I can just get a message to them, they might be able to pass it on to Molly somehow. Then she can let me know if she's OK.

I find a list of all the government space agencies around the world, and track down the coordinates of their antennas, satellites, and space stations orbiting Earth. It's a long shot—some of the organizations might not exist at all anymore, or might have shut down their operations because of the war too—but I can't just sit here and do nothing. I would never forgive myself if I didn't even try.

***

From: The Infinity Sent: 03/24/2067

To: ESA; ISRO; CNSA; Predicted date of receipt: 12/05/2068

JAXA; RFSA; AEM; APSCO;

UKSA; ISA; ASI; KCST; KARI;

CNES

Subject: FAO Dr. Molly Simmons—URGENT

Dear Sir/Madam,

This is Commander Romy Silvers, broadcasting from the NASA spacecraft *The Infinity*. I am transmitting this message to Earth in the hope of reaching someone who is still scanning for signals from deep space.

I wish to be put in contact with Dr. Molly Simmons, an employee at NASA who used to be in charge of my communications with Earth. I have received no information about her whereabouts, and since the war started she might have relocated, but I know that she is a trained psychologist and therapist with a degree from Harvard University. Her sister is a general posted at the military base on Antarctica. She has a cat called Nino.

If there's any way for you to determine the current location of Dr. Simmons and send her this message, I would be very grateful. I would like to know whether she is safe during the conflict on Earth.

I will be forever in your debt if you could grant me this favor.

Yours faithfully,

Commander R. Silvers

Message to Dr. Molly Simmons as follows:

Molly,

I really hope you get this message. I'm completely out of other ideas for how to speak to you.

I'm so worried about you, and I just can't stand not knowing whether you're safe anymore. Are you OK? Please, please be OK.

I hope your sister is safe too. I hope she's not fighting in the war, or at least that she's not on the front line.

More than anything, I just want to hear from you again. I've been very lucky, as I have Commander Shoreditch of *The Eternity* to talk to. His support has been incredible. But I miss you so much it hurts.

Stay safe, for me.

Romy x

I stay up late writing fic, practicing the piano on the helm's touchscreen, and basically doing anything possible to avoid going to sleep. I can't have another dream about the astronauts. I can't handle that, not on top of everything else.

I've had the nightmares since I was four, when we lost the astronauts. The sight of hundreds of corpses has been impossible to erase from my mind. I don't really remember a time before the astronauts began to haunt my nights.

Dad used to let me sleep in his bunk in those early days when my mother wasn't sleeping at all. When she just stayed in the sick bay, trying and failing to fix what had gone wrong.

Some nights, Dad would wake up screaming from nightmares too. I think that made it worse. For everything else that upset me, Dad was there to make it better. A problem with the ship? He knew what to do. A headache or injury? He could fix it.

But the astronauts—they scared him too. They scared him more than they did me. That left me petrified. If my incredible, brave, genius father was helpless against them, then what hope did I have?

There was nothing to be done back then but wait it out.

All three of us tried our best. I suppose the lingering nightmares are a small price to pay for what happened to them. I got off lightly, compared with my mother.

I wake up shivering at five in the morning to find myself still at the helm, my head pillowed on my arms and a fic open on the computer. Line after line of Js fill the page. I must have fallen asleep with my head touching the keyboard, typing Jayden's name.

jjjjjjjjjjjjjjjjjjjjjjjjjjjjjjjjjjjjjjjjjjjjjjjjjjjjjjjjjjjjjjjjjjjjjjjjjjjjjjjjjjjjjjjjjjjjjj

I delete the letters and go to my bunk.

DAYS UNTIL *THE ETERNITY* ARRIVES:
330

From: The Eternity

To: The Infinity

Sent: 10/10/2065

Received: 04/01/2067

Commander Silvers,

I'm writing because I don't know what else to do anymore. I've spent the last few months wishing and hoping that NASA will get back in touch with us. But it looks like the DSN communications aren't going to be reinstated for a while yet.

I'm at a loss. I can't stop thinking about my friends. They're all stuck on Earth in the middle of a war, and I can't even make sure they are safe. I don't know if they are in a war zone or not.

Although it's only supposed to be an official communication line for emergencies, I'm really glad I can at least speak with you, Commander Silvers. If you don't mind, I think I might send you more frequent messages from now on. I don't know whether you'll welcome these messages, but seeing as you can't tell me one way or another just yet, I'm going to keep talking to you anyway. Feel free to ignore my chatter or not, as you wish.

Whatever happens on Earth, at least it won't affect our actual ships. Not even the largest nuclear bombs can stretch this far, I hope.

Commander Shoreditch (but you can call me J. We might as well drop the formalities at this point, don't you think, Romy?)

From: The Infinity   Sent: 04/01/2067
To: The Eternity   Predicted date of receipt: 06/30/2067

J,

I'm so sorry. It never even occurred to me that you wouldn't have heard from your family and friends since the war started. I hope this war ends soon, for your sake more than my own.

Of course you can talk to me, if it will help you. It would be comforting for me too. We can be interstellar pen pals.

Romy

I keep catching myself gazing into nothing, hands loose at my sides. I've got a horrible feeling that I'm falling into a trap, but I can't work out what kind of trap it could possibly be.

I'm sure it's just paranoia. My brain is playing tricks on me, in the same way it always does whenever I see a flicker of light and become certain that there's someone just around the corner, watching me.

The war can't hurt me. I'm only a bystander. It's not my prob-lem. Whatever "nuclear bombs" Commander Shoreditch—J—thinks are being let off on Earth, they can't touch me here.

My brain doesn't seem to want to listen. I've got that famil-iar worry about everything going wrong. I need to make sure I'm ready. I need to know how everything on *The Infinity* works, in case there's an emergency. I'm on my own now, at least until *The Eternity* catches up.

If I get ill, there will be no one to help me. No one to fix me if I break. I try to ease my worries by giving myself a medical exam. I take my pulse, my temperature, and my glucose levels using a urine sample.

The readouts tell me that I'm fine. I can't quite believe them. I decide to start checking myself every week. I can't get ill. I need to be OK.

DAYS UNTIL *THE ETERNITY* ARRIVES:
328

From: The Eternity   Sent: 10/18/2065

To: The Infinity   Received: 04/03/2067

Dear Romy,

It's harder than I thought it would be to talk to a person who can't reply. I'm not really sure what to write about. I suppose the best place to start, if we are actually going to get to know each other, is to tell you about myself. If nothing else, that should make our first meeting a little less awkward.

Here's a short history of Commander J Shoreditch. I'm a twenty-two-year-old male. I studied medicine at college. In my second year, I decided that I just couldn't spend another three years studying, so I did the obvious thing and applied for a job at NASA.

At the time, they were looking for trainee astronauts to prepare for the new mission. I somehow conned my way into the position, probably helped by the fact that the program director was an alumnus of my college. I am perfectly willing to take advantage of my privilege.

I'm pretty honored to be chosen, even though my entire job is to grow old in space, as a caretaker in the service of humanity.

Which brings us up to today, which I spent marathoning an entire season of a TV show. Clearly I have quite the illustrious career.

You're writing back, aren't you? I hope you are. That would make this whole sending-messages-to-a-stranger thing a lot less weird. I can't believe you won't read this message for over a year. I feel like I'm talking to the future.

J

J is only twenty-two! That's so much younger than I was expecting. I suppose it makes sense to send out young astronauts, so they aren't old by the time we reach Earth II, but still—twenty-two. That's only a few years older than me.

No wonder it's so easy to talk to him. We're peers. I've never had a peer before. And twenty-two is close enough to my age that it's not—

I mean, it's a bit weird, but . . . Jayden was only twenty-two in Series 1 of *Loch & Ness*, when Lyra was nineteen. That's almost the same age difference as between me and J, plus or minus a few years. OK, three years.

But still. It's close. Close enough for— I don't even let

myself think what for.

My body suddenly feels too big for me, too grown-up and strong for the young girl inside it. I'm not ready to be this person, in this situation. I can't think about this. I refuse.

It's enough just to know how old he is for now. J is twenty-two, a boy, clever and funny—and, best of all, apparently interested in talking to *me*. It's flattering in a confusing, lovely way.

From: The Infinity   Sent: 04/03/2067
To: The Eternity   Predicted date of receipt: 07/02/2067

J,

I'm so glad you finally told me about yourself. I had been wondering who you were. It's amazing that you're only twenty-two and you're an astronaut. That's so impressive.

I'm not really sure what to tell you about myself in return, but here are some facts about me.

- I've never met anyone who wasn't related to me.
- I'm never going to see planet Earth.
- I'm the only person to have ever been born in space. (I know you know this one already. But this is the only interesting thing about me! I'm really boring, honestly.)
- I love writing.
- I can tell you more things I've never done than things I have done.

Romy

DAYS UNTIL *THE ETERNITY* ARRIVES:
327

Today, in my endless search for every bit of data from Earth that I have saved on my hard drive, I somehow found myself looking through the old security footage from the ship. Recordings from years ago are still archived, stretching all the way back to when I was a baby. From before everything went wrong.

I find a clip of Dad in *The Infinity*'s kitchen, feeding me some kind of mashed-up food and cooing to me gently. The cameras are in the ceiling, so the angle is too high to see our faces—just the tops of our heads in the corner of the picture. The rest of the shot captures the curve of the clean white wall, the chrome fittings shining in the fluorescent lights.

I can tell that I'm happy. My chubby arms wave around, knocking the baby food across my high chair. Dad tips his head back and laughs. I can make out the wrinkles at the corners of his eyes. My heart bumps.

He leans over and kisses my forehead before he starts cleaning up.

I watch until the door slides open as my mother enters the room and starts talking to Dad. She's smiling.

Suddenly the ache in my throat is gone. Here is my mother, smiling, laughing, joking. This is what my parents' marriage must have been like, when my mother could look at Dad and me without seeing the faces of the astronauts.

She looks like a different person. Contented and carefree. The recording shows me the mother I might have had, if things had been different.

I close down the file, feeling worse than I did before.

DAYS UNTIL *THE ETERNITY* ARRIVES:
322

From: The Eternity   Sent: 11/07/2065
To: The Infinity   Received: 04/09/2067

Romy,

I've been trying to imagine what kind of messages you're sending me. Presuming that you are, and that you're being friendly, I've come up with a few questions you might have asked. So I'm going to answer your hypothetical questions. That way you don't have to wait months for answers!

What do you look like?

I've got brown hair and brown eyes and all of my teeth. I'm five foot nine.

When's your birthday?

In seven months, twenty days on June 27. Hope you got me something nice!

What do you think Earth II will be like?

I have no idea. That seems so far off that I've not even thought about it yet. I like the two suns. I've been running simulations during my training and it all looks kind of like a giant desert.

Speaking of the training—is yours as algebraic as mine? I thought we were supposed to be starting a new civilization, not solving Fermat's last theorem!

Before the launch, NASA Earth told me that you've been studying astrophysics since you were eight. That's really impressive, Romy. I can't believe you're only sixteen and you're at the same level as I am. You're really cool.

Do you miss your family?

I don't really have much family. Both of my parents died when I was young. You don't need to tell me that you're sorry or anything—it's not your fault, right? Anyway, it was a long time ago. Though time doesn't really make any difference to pain. It never disappears.

I still catch myself making a note of scandalous things to tell my mom (she was a really big gossip). I still remember the smell of my father's cologne.

I still get unbelievably angry when I think about how young they were when they died. It's so unfair that preventable things happen to good people, just through carelessness. That pain hasn't dulled at all.

Anyway, the answer to my self-asked question is that I always miss my family, but that's nothing new.

What's your favorite animal?

Seals. Whenever I get sad, I watch videos of seals on YouTube. They're basically mermaid dogs, and they are all giant idiots. I love them.

What should I do about my [miscellaneous illness]?

Take some penicillin and/or vitamins. I told you, I dropped out of college after two years. I can't help you much.

So . . . was I close? Are these the questions you've been asking? Was I even in the vicinity of being close? Do you care about my life at all?

J

I've got really bad period pains today, so I decide to make a blanket fort. I balance blankets over the top of the lounge area so that the sofa, set into the floor, turns into a tiny, comfy cocoon.

The fabric tinges the light a peaceful shade of pink, and I curl up inside my fort and listen to the softest classical music I can find. I reread all of J's emails, one after the other, coming back again and again to the description of what he looks like, from today's email.

Brown hair and eyes. Five foot nine.

I sketch a doodle of how I picture him in my head. He comes out looking like Jayden Ness, with a mess of tight curls on his head, and long eyelashes surrounding eyes filled with warmth. He's smiling a bright, brilliant smile, one hand raised in a wave.

I carefully tape it to the wall next to my bunk so I can look at it before I go to sleep. With J *and* Jayden to look at, I feel safer. Like they're watching over me.

From: The Infinity   Sent: 04/09/2067
To: The Eternity   Predicted date of receipt: 07/05/2067

J,

Your last message was like seeing inside my own head. The way you feel about your parents—that's exactly how I feel about mine too. It's like you've been reading my diary. (I don't write a diary, but still.)

I really am sorry they died, even though you told me not to say that. You don't deserve to have had such a horrible thing happen to you. I can't stop thinking about you being left alone like that. I just want to go back in time and give you the biggest, warmest hug you've ever had.

How did they die? Did you decide to apply for *The Eternity*'s mission because of their deaths? You don't have to tell me if it's too raw. I still can't even think about my parents' deaths, let alone talk about them. It just—it feels less real if I don't focus on the details.

On a lighter note, happy belated birthday for . . . last year. Ahem. Well, it's the thought that counts. Maybe this message will get to you by your next birthday instead.

Happy 23rd/24th/25th birthday! [delete as applicable]

You did answer some of the questions I was wondering about,

thank you. That made talking to you with this long delay a bit less frustrating.

I have one other question for you—what do you look like? In my head I keep picturing you like Jayden Ness from *Loch & Ness*. The way you described yourself sounded a bit like him, and he was studying to be a doctor too before he joined the supernatural police. (Plus Jayden is a selkie, so he turns into a seal, your favorite animal!)

Also, I have to admit that I'm not the physics genius you've been told. Ever since my parents died, I've been finding it really hard to do any calculations at all. Every time I try, my brain just seizes up.

It sounds like maybe you felt the same way, when you stopped studying medicine. Did you quit because the pressure made it hard for you to focus? How did you fix that when you joined NASA? I've tried everything, and nothing works. I'd love some tips.

R

DAYS UNTIL *THE ETERNITY* ARRIVES:
319

Today the computer alerts me that the annual maintenance tasks for the ship are overdue.

Dad and I used to do them together. He would make it into a game, asking me to hand him tools as if I was his assistant. We would do the more simple things first, like recalibrating the thermal management system to the correct temperature for the life support, and cleaning the filters of the thrust boosters. When I got bored and went off to play, he'd do the difficult jobs.

We used to carry our lunches with us and take long breaks to eat them, even though it would have taken all of five minutes to go back to the kitchen—the ship isn't very large. But Dad said that was missing the point of a good old-fashioned picnic. We would sit on the floor in the corridor and eat sandwiches, sipping lukewarm tea from a thermos.

Once, my mother came across us while we were eating our picnic. By the time I was about nine, she tended to keep to herself. I hadn't seen her in weeks. I remember she just looked at us. I could tell she had absolutely no idea what we were doing, or why—even though she'd been the one to teach me about the importance of maintaining the ship in the first place, back when we created our model of *The Infinity*. When she saw us sitting there, she just turned and walked away. Dad stopped talking midsentence. I touched his arm, but he looked at me like he'd forgotten what we were doing there too.

That memory hurts. We'd already lost her, and I didn't even know it.

When I find myself staring into space, I shake myself and go back to reading through the computer's instructions for the first task. I need to replace a circuit board that is running on lowered efficiency in the sun room.

I use the 3D printer to make a new board, and open up the back panel of the UV light. Using a small screwdriver, I swap the old board for the new.

A memory I didn't know I had appears in my mind: following my mother around while she changed a circuit board in a door lock. I must have only been four. I remember tugging on her overalls, begging her to play with me. I remember her grabbing my arms and pulling me away from an open panel.

"Don't touch the wires, Romy," she said. "They'll shock you."

It's an old memory, so faint that only the physical act of

replacing wires manages to bring it to the forefront of my mind. Forcing myself to think of something else instead, I start writing a new fic in my head.

I imagine a story where Jayden works in a bookshop. He'd probably wear a Fair Isle sweater vest and those sexy, thick-rimmed glasses that clever characters always seem to wear. He'd lounge lazily across the counter as he made book recommendations to customers. Everyone who'd come into the bookshop would leave slightly stunned, with the beginnings of a crush. He wouldn't even notice because he'd be too busy pining after the cute girl who would go to the bookshop to buy a romance novel every single Wednesday lunchtime. Jayden would probably change his shifts to make sure he was there when she came in. Once, when she didn't turn up, he panicked and asked all the other customers whether they knew if she was OK.

I move from one job to the next, replacing air filters, cleaning solar panels and telescope lenses, lubricating joints in the boiler and the water recycling unit, then checking the pressure of the liquid oxygen tanks. I don't find any major problems. The ship has been working for years without anything going wrong.

I ignore the voice in the back of my head that never leaves, telling me *nothing has gone wrong* yet. When it does, it will be up to me to notice it. NASA used to monitor the system data, which is regularly transmitted back to Earth, but now the war has started there's no one analyzing the data except me.

My final task is to remove static from the ship by cleaning up the charged particles of dust that cover each surface. The air filtration automatically picks up most of the dust, but there's always places where it clings determinedly. If the dust built up, the static could cause a fire, so I have to check everywhere myself, just to be safe.

I wander around with a duster, getting into all the nooks and crevices of the floors and walls. When I reach the gene bank, I check that the panel on the door is green, which means that everything is fine with the terrible cryopreserved human spawn inside.

The room contains one thousand cryogenically frozen human embryos, eggs and sperm samples, taken from loads of different countries on Earth before the ship launched. It was supposed to be a secondary source of DNA, to guarantee genetic diversity on Earth II. Now that the astronauts are gone, the embryos will be the only way that we can establish a colony on Earth II. Without the samples, this whole journey would be pointless.

The embryos will stay in long-term cryogenic storage until the ship gets nearer to Earth II. Then I'll have to set up an enormous artificial womb in the labs. It will incubate a few of the embryos until they are fully grown babies.

There was supposed to be a whole community of astronauts to adopt the children. Instead I'm going to be responsible for raising an entire generation, to make sure that there are people to work on Earth II and make it livable. It has a hospitable atmosphere—oxygen, water, nitrogen . . . all of the essentials—but we'll still need to build housing and set up agriculture. There'll be a lot to do.

I could start off an embryo now and bring up the first baby, if I wanted to. Maybe I would have, if J hadn't been sent to save me. Luckily, *The Infinity* will have joined up with *The Eternity* long before we need to start caring for children.

With any luck, J knows how to burp a baby. I'm not exactly qualified. I can barely even look after myself.

I'm running the duster along the edges of the floor in the corridor when I find it. It's leaning against the inner edge of the doorframe of the gene bank, tucked neatly up by the wall. It's so tiny that it isn't a surprise I've missed it all these years.

It's a shard from some kind of metallic container; a curved fragment of a larger cylinder, broken unevenly along a fracture line. I only notice it at all because the sharp edge catches the side of my thumb.

When my fingers touch the roughness of the engraving, I realize immediately what it must be. Slowly, I turn it over to see the letters:

vers, M.D.

Gasping, I drop it like I've been burned.

Dr. Silvers, M.D. It's a fragment of the oxygen tank from my mother's spacesuit.

I thought I'd found them all. I'd been so careful, all those years ago. I never wanted to see any reminder of my mother ever again. But apparently I missed this shard, lingering at the scene of the crime like evidence waiting to be found.

I can taste the sour tang of vomit in the back of my throat. I have to get rid of it. Now. Just knowing that it is on the ship, on *my ship*, makes me shudder.

I tuck it into my palm so I don't have to look at it, feeling the metal leach the warmth from my skin, and walk as fast as I can to the airlock.

The seal hisses when I pull open the inner door of the pressurized airlock. I step into the chamber set into the hull of the spaceship. Through a porthole in the outer door, I can see straight out into space. If I opened that door now, I'd be dead in less than a minute as the vacuum pulled the air from my chest, taking my lungs along with it.

I don't.

Instead I place the shard on the floor of the chamber, and return to the safety of my ship, closing the inner door. Looking through the window, the fragment seems harmless. It's impossible to imagine the damage it caused.

I swallow, hard. I seal the airlock, and the system pumps to remove the air from the chamber.

In my mind, I watch the tank break, the way I have time and time again since it first happened.

I'd forgotten how cold it was against skin. I'd forgotten how shiny the steel looked when it was covered in blood.

The outer door of the airlock slides open in a silent, easy motion. The last remaining piece of my mother's oxygen tank slips out into space. I catch a flash of light gleaming off its surface before it's left behind in the wake of the ship.

Gone.

DAYS UNTIL *THE ETERNITY* ARRIVES:
314

From: The Eternity

Sent: 11/30/2065

To: The Infinity

Received: 04/17/2067

Attachment: L&N.zip [3 GB]

Good morning, Romy,

I have some questions for you today, since I was so considerate as to answer yours. Even if yours were hypothetical and uninvited, it still counts. Promise.

Why do you like *Loch & Ness* so much? (I've attached the rest of the latest season, by the way. Enjoy!)

Even if the journey takes another nineteen years, would you turn the ship around and go back to Earth if you could?

I wonder a lot about what life is like for you, alone on your ship. You don't have to tell me anything you don't want to, but I'd like to hear about it.

J

J,

Interesting questions.

I like *Loch & Ness* because it's the complete opposite of my life. I've rewatched it so many times that the characters feel like real friends to me. Jayden is my favorite. He acts like he's really cool and jokes around a lot, but actually he's a total sweetheart. He's hilarious too, and completely in love with Lyra, even though she doesn't know that yet.

As to your second question, I actually did try to go back to Earth just after my parents died. I was all on my own, so I panicked and did what my eleven-year-old brain thought NASA would want me to do. I tried to turn the ship around.

You probably know that it's not like turning a car around—it takes years and years to turn a spaceship around, obviously. You've had all the real astronaut training. Well, I didn't have any of that. I thought it would be easy. I thought I'd be able to go back to Earth and let someone else take over the mission.

I'd also gotten really fixated on my dad's dad, who was still alive at that point. All I could think about was going back to Earth and meeting my granddad for the first time. I thought he could adopt me. I knew that by the time I got back to Earth I'd be thirty, and wouldn't need adopting, but I just ignored that. I was in denial.

Anyway, I marched up to the helm one day, hands on my hips,

and ordered the computer to turn the ship around. It refused. I pressed a lot of buttons and did a lot of shouting, and it was still like, "No."

Because I didn't have the command codes, it wouldn't give me access. It forced me to stay away from the controls until I'd calmed down—which took a good few months.

I think it was only when Molly started talking to me that I finally accepted I couldn't go home. (Did you talk to Molly too, from NASA? Isn't she just the best? I miss her more than anything else, now that the transmissions are down.)

In her first message, she promoted my authorization codes to make me the commander of *The Infinity*. I realized I could actually turn the ship around. So I tried again.

I got pretty far with it. I set up the instructions and coordinates and even ordered more fuel to be sent to the thrusters. But when I went to press the button, I just couldn't do it.

I think it was because this person at NASA was giving *me* total control of a spaceship. Me, Romy Silvers. I was only fourteen, but I was really in charge. That made me realize how serious it was. They were all relying on me.

Our ships are about more than just us, aren't they? Everyone on Earth is depending on us to get to Earth II. They've invested nearly half a century of money, time, and research into getting us there. I couldn't let them down just because I was scared.

I couldn't change what had happened to my parents. I couldn't change the fact that I was here, and that I was always going to be here, and my parents weren't. So I just got on with it. This voyage was never meant to be easy. It was meant to be important.

Anyway, that's enough of that, or it'll spoil my appetite—and I've got tomato soup for dinner to look forward to! (That's my favorite.)

That turned out a lot longer than I thought it would. Sorry if it got more emotional than you were expecting! There's something about you that just makes me want to open up, I think.

R

PS Thank you so much for the rest of *Loch & Ness.* I know what my plans are for the rest of the day . . . !

DAYS UNTIL *THE ETERNITY* ARRIVES:
293

I spend the morning making a model house out of dinner packets. I carefully cut little doors and windows out of the plastic, trying to remember what the flat-pack buildings in the stores look like so I can copy the design. I want to make houses similar to the ones J and I will be living in on Earth II. Then I'll be able to picture what our lives will be like.

I keep finding myself daydreaming about how my first meeting with J will go. Will we hug? Will talking be as easy as emailing is, or will it be really awkward?

Today is the two-month anniversary of the last time I heard from Earth. It's possible—maybe even likely—that J and I are the only two human beings left in the entire universe. Earth could have blown itself up, destroying every single life-form on the planet, and we would have no idea.

Even if we did, there's nothing that we could do about it. We would just have to . . . keep going. The idea is almost freeing.

Ever since I lost contact with Earth, J's messages have become so precious. It started out as a nice bonus on top of Molly's audio clips, but now we send each other emails daily, and his messages are the highlight of my day. Seeing a new message from him makes my pulse jump in excitement.

At least something good has come from the war. It's brought us closer together.

DAYS UNTIL *THE ETERNITY* ARRIVES:
292

From: The Eternity

To: The Infinity

Sent: 02/08/2066

Received: 05/09/2067

Romy,

What do you do every day on your spaceship? I've only been here for seven months and I've already done nearly everything from my list of things I've wanted to do for years, which is basically:

- Sleep
- Game for ten hours straight
- Practice juggling
- Manage to deadlift 200 kg, finally
- Run 18 km at a 5-minute pace

The only thing I haven't managed to do is learn to juggle, which I've decided—after a few attempts—was a terrible idea, and something no sane person should ever try. I keep dropping the balls everywhere and setting off the ship's impact alarms. I think I'm too clumsy for hobbies that involve throwing objects around at high speed.

It's a shame, because I've wanted to learn to juggle since I was in college. Once, I was talking to a girl in my class and I bragged that I could do it. My roommate was listening and he called me on it, and told me to prove it. I ended up giving myself a black eye. Obviously, the girl didn't give me her number.

I got my revenge on my roommate, though. I used to pull lots of pranks. I was always covering the toilet seat in plastic wrap or ordering a dozen pizzas to be delivered to people who hadn't ordered them. I definitely made my friend regret the juggling incident.

It was funny at the time, but looking back now, it's just embarrassing. I was awful when I was eighteen.

To get back to the point: I've checked everything off my to-do list. Now I'm kind of lying around aimlessly, which is fine, I guess. I wasn't expecting endless entertainment or anything. I know I'm not going to be waiting for nearly as long as you've been. A couple of years is nothing compared with a lifetime!

J

From: The Infinity
To: The Eternity

Sent: 05/09/2067
Predicted date of receipt: 07/25/2067

Good morning, J,

I can't believe you're already bored. You've got a hard few years ahead of you! Not that I can talk. You're basically the most interesting thing in my life, especially now that you've sent me the rest of the *Loch & Ness* episodes. (Please say you've started watching it? Because that series finale! I really need to discuss it with you!) And like I said, you really remind me of Jayden. It's funny how similar you two are. It's such a coincidence.

I learned to juggle when I was ten. It's manageable if you start with two balls and build up. I should try it again sometime so I can give you tips.

I love that you pulled pranks at university. That's really cute.

My dad always used to tell me stories about his time at university. He was British, and he studied at the University of Cambridge, where he was headhunted by NASA. My mother was American, and he met her in the orientation sessions at NASA. But before they met, when he was studying, I think he had a lot of girlfriends. His stories always had different girls in them.

I think you would've liked my dad. I wish you could have met him.

I'd like to have wild stories about my university days to tell my kids, someday. I'd like to have any anecdotes at all, actually. I used to wish that if I ever fell for someone, it would start with a funny little meet-cute that would make a nice story.

Obviously that's not going to happen, seeing as I have literally no dating prospects at all, living in the endless vacuum of space, but I was a delusional kid. I had a lot of imagination.

R

DAYS UNTIL *THE ETERNITY* ARRIVES:
274

From: The Eternity

To: The Infinity

Sent: 04/04/2066

Received: 05/27/2067

Romy,

I'm really surprised by how much I miss Earth. I didn't expect it to be so bad, because when I was on Earth I spent every day desperate to just start the mission already.

I have nothing to be anything but happy about, but I keep getting these horrible pangs in my gut out of nowhere. Every time, it takes me a while to realize that it's because I'm homesick. I just want to be outside.

I never knew how much I need the sky, or the ground, or wind.

Here are the things I miss most about home, now that I've been away for nearly ten months:

- Walking aimlessly in any direction I want and never

running up against a wall or circling back on myself

- The texture of wood (everything here is made of plastic or metal, or plastic-coated metal)
- Real, paper books, with pages and ink, and spines that you can crack
- Hot baths
- The smell of perfume in a girl's hair
- Everything about girls in general: their laughs, and smiles, and soft skin, and—OK, I'm officially censoring myself with this one. Sorry.
- Dogs
- Sitting at a bar with condensation from a cold glass dripping over my fingers
- Getting properly, seriously drunk. I've had to find all these new ways to relax without beer.
- The sound of rain against the windowpanes in the morning, when you just wake up and know you don't have to get up for at least an hour
- Birdsong

I can't stop thinking about taking you to Earth, even though that's never going to happen. I'd love to watch your face the first time you saw snow, or stroked a kitten. It's like I'm understanding everything differently now because I'm looking at it from your perspective. I want to see your reaction to everything, from the rare to the commonplace.

I'm really enjoying writing to you, Romy. I've never had a pen pal before. I had a girlfriend in college who used to make me write her during the holidays—but I think that was just so she could show off to her friends about the letters her boyfriend had sent her. She never wrote back.

J x

From: The Infinity   Sent: 05/27/2067
To: The Eternity   Predicted date of receipt: 08/05/2067
Attachment: Relaxation-tapes.mp3 [4 MB]

J,

I wish I really could visit Earth with you. That sounds heavenly. Obviously I've never been to Earth, so I can't tell you what I miss, but I can tell you what I want to experience the most:

- Group hugs with friends
- Narrowly avoiding being run over by traffic on a New York street
- Popcorn and Slush Puppies at the cinema
- Candles! What are they about?
- Getting to play a real, actual piano instead of an electric keyboard
- Quicksand—how often do you usually get stuck in this stuff? A few times a month? It seems to happen all the time in films!
- Daisy chains
- Spiderwebs
- Climbing trees and looking into birds' nests

- Beer. I've never been drunk. I can't really work out what it's like. Is it similar to when you wake up from a really great dream, and for a moment you can't remember what's real life and what are your subconscious's darkest desires, and everything's a bit hazy? That's what I imagine it's like, anyway.
- THE SEA. SWIMMING POOLS. BATHS. What's it like, floating in water? It sounds scary.

I think mostly I just want to meet you, though. I could stand missing Earth if I got to see you in person.

R x

PS After I read your email I searched through the video archives and found some recordings of birdsong and rain. The minute the birdsong started playing, I immediately felt calmer. My brain must be hardwired to find the sound peaceful, even though I've never heard a bird in real life. No wonder you love it so much.

I'm sending over the recordings, so you can listen to them whenever you feel homesick. I've set the rainfall as my morning alarm tune, so it will be like we're together, listening to the same rain outside our windows.

When I think about all of the possibilities that could have been, I feel sick. If the war had broken out before *The Eternity* was launched, I would have been left alone. I would have been completely abandoned, without J for company.

I got so lucky. In what could have been the worst, most isolating time of my life, I've been given the best friendship. It's like it was fate, like J was sent to guide me through the darkness to keep me sane.

Without J, I would be nothing. I'd be less than nothing— I'd be forgotten. J cares about me. J is here for me, now that no one else is. He even put a kiss at the end of his email. A kiss, to me!

I hesitate before I send the message, and reread the part about having never been drunk. It makes me seem immature. *Everyone* has tried alcohol in films. Characters get drunk all the time, like it's nothing. J will think I'm a baby for not knowing what that's like.

I delete that paragraph before I send the email.

That evening, I find myself opening Dad's locker to stare at his bottle of whiskey. It's in an expensive-looking box: black with embossed gold writing. It's double my age.

Dad was saving it for when we landed on the new planet. The crew weren't allowed to bring many personal items on board with them, but this was one of his. My mother chose to bring her sewing supplies with her.

I take the bottle to the kitchen and pour a glass of the golden liquid. I might as well put the alcohol to good use. It will be interesting to know what being drunk feels like, just for future reference. J might mention it again.

DAYS UNTIL *THE ETERNITY* ARRIVES:
273

Before I'm even awake, I wish I were asleep again. A sharp pain shoots across my skull when I breathe in and out. My eyelashes are gloopy with sleep, and I can actually *hear* the blood pounding in my ears. It's too loud.

What *happened* to me?

The last thing I remember is trying to decide whether the whiskey might taste less awful if I added ice. Since then, something terrible must have happened. There's a swarm of wasps inside my skull, buzzing angrily. I feel like I'm dying. I've definitely caught a horrific disease. A flesh-eating fungus of some kind.

I don't have the energy to panic just yet, though. First I need to sleep for ten years. I rub my eyelids, trying to summon the energy to get up and brush my teeth. My mouth feels fuzzy.

This can't be the hangover that all the films talk about. It just can't. It's too terrible. If this is the result of drinking, then why would anyone bother?

A flash of last night crosses my mind: me, sprawled over the side of the sofa, maniacally singing show tunes and slurping whiskey through a straw from a glass on the floor.

Oh. That's why.

I lever myself into a sitting position and venture into the bathroom to try and find an aspirin.

The living area is a complete mess. I seem to have taken every single item out of the cabinets. The sofa cushions are scattered across the room, as if I was making stepping stones to play a game of The Floor Is Lava—the way I used to with Dad.

Groaning, I dry-swallow a pill and drop back into my bunk. I cannot deal with the mess right now. I don't even want to see the state of the kitchen—I have vague memories of attempting to make a four-layer sandwich.

I go back to sleep.

Drunk Romy did come up with a great obstacle course made out of mushroom-soup boxes to jump over in the corridor while running. So I guess she's not the worst ever.

I'm still going to drink less whiskey next time, though.

DAYS UNTIL *THE ETERNITY* ARRIVES:
266

I spend the morning making origami farm animals to add to the yard of my food-container model house. Carefully folding lines of brown and white paper into chickens, pigs, horses, and cows, I place them around my farm in groups of two and three. I think I might save up packaging so that I can make a barn for them—and maybe another farmhouse. I could make a pond out of foil, and some origami ducks, if I can find a pattern for them.

I'm so busy crafting that it's midafternoon before I notice the new email in my inbox:

From: Earth   Sent: 09/19/2065
To: The Infinity   Received: 06/04/2067

There's an enormous noise in my ears. I think it's my own heart-beat, pounding like an alarm.

A message. From Molly? It must be.

I stare at the message, suddenly terrified to open it. I don't know why, but I feel sick. I've been waiting for this moment for months. Now that it's here, I wish it wasn't.

My vision rattles, shuddering along with my breathing. Everything feels balanced on the head of a pin. What if it's bad news? What if something has happened to Molly?

I was finally getting used to being out of contact with Earth. I was feeling happy again.

I have to open the message; I know I do. I want to. But what if it's a mistake? What if the computer glitched and there's really no new message at all? I brace myself for the worst.

I click.

A page of text fills the screen. It takes me longer than it should to work out why I can't read it: it's in a different language, with an unfamiliar alphabet.

I pull up a translator, pasting the text into it and waiting for the message to process into English.

From: Earth   Sent: 09/19/2065
To: The Infinity   Received: 06/04/2067
Subject: For Attention of The Infinity

Dear Sir/Madam,
Note: This message is intended for Commander R. Silvers of Earth vessel *The Infinity*. If it arrives at a time that Commander Silvers is no longer in office, this message should

be relayed to her successor.

We are writing to inform you that *The Infinity* and the transmission unit on Earth are now in the control of our noble Union of the People's Republic. The United States of America was disbanded on July 2, 2065, and the countries of North America have been absorbed into the UPR, together with all scientific government organizations.

We would welcome you as a fresh citizen and representative of the UPR from these moments on, and have large hopes for *The Infinity* and *The Eternity* missions.

Since last contacted, the political landscape of Earth has shifted a considerable amount by the powerful UPR's victory in the Third Global War. Regardless, we hope *The Infinity* had no similar disruption and is still operating smoothly.

The UPR is in the process of installing new antennas to detect messages, one of the original having been destroyed in the bombing of Europe. We look forward to receiving *The Infinity* communications at your pleasure in the future, and eagerly await a confirmation that *The Infinity* is still on course to reach the destination Planet HT 3485 c.

All hail the UPR! May the king live long and vigorously!

I don't— I can't— This doesn't make sense. I can't even—*what*?

Bombing of Europe?

Molly. Is she OK? Is she still alive? The message doesn't say. Molly could be dead and I would have no idea.

This is my worst nightmare come to life. I can't keep hold of the thoughts running through my mind. As soon as I try to focus, everything scatters out of my grasp. I make myself stop thinking about Molly, using the methods she taught me to calm down. If I carry on panicking, I'll be destroyed completely.

I run through everything, trying to process it all objectively.

NASA has been taken over by another government. I don't know how to feel about that. I want to be happy that I'm getting messages from Earth again at all, regardless of who is sending them.

It's not like I've ever even been to Earth. I have no real investment in which ruling government is currently controlling the piece of land that one of my parents came from—or that the land the other came from has been bombed. It's all happening on a planet I've never seen. But I still feel uneasy.

I read the message over and over. The words feel like a vise, clenching around my heart. It might just be the translation, making the message come out odd and unemotional. It must be hard for software to translate tone accurately. If I could read the original language, it would probably be a great message, really welcoming and friendly.

The UPR are probably nice people. The next message I get from them will be totally normal.

But if the war ended in July, then why did it take them until September to get in touch?

I drop onto the sofa and then seconds later jump up again

in favor of pacing the room.

I don't think I'm being told the whole story.

Suddenly I feel lonelier than before the message arrived.

I miss Molly.

I need to talk to J.

From: The Infinity   Sent: 06/04/2067
To: The Eternity   Predicted date of receipt: 08/10/2067

J,

Did you get an email from Earth? From something called the UPR?

It's the worst message I've ever received—even worse than the last message from my friend Molly. I'm so scared.

I need to know what's happening. I need to know if Molly is still alive. What can we do? Is there *anything* we can do? Or do we just have to sit here, waiting, like always?

I don't trust them, J. Nothing they are saying makes any sense. They are lying to us. I'm so glad you're here. I'm so glad there's someone I can rely on.

R x

From: The Eternity   Sent: 04/30/2066
To: The Infinity   Received: 06/04/2067

Romy,

I guess by now you've picked up the message from the "UPR" too. As soon as I read it, I messaged you. I didn't want you to have to deal with their email without hearing from me—but I don't really know how I feel yet. Sorry if this sounds a bit confused.

It's just all so strange. I want to be angry. I *should* be angry. This dictatorship has taken over my country. I should hate them, right? I should, but (and I would never normally admit this, especially not to a girl) I'm scared, Romy.

There's nothing I can do about it. There's no way that I can help my friends.

I don't know what I'd do if you weren't here too. Probably turn the ship around and go back to Earth like a one-man army. I'd try to save them all and get blown up in the process. I can't believe it.

J x

DAYS UNTIL *THE ETERNITY* ARRIVES:
261

From: UPR   Sent: 09/23/2065

To: The Infinity   Received: 06/09/2067

Subject: For Attention of The Infinity

Attachment: Antenna-coordinates.txt [40 KB]

Commander Silvers,

We hope everything is well on *The Infinity* and there is no reason for concern with regard to the progress of the vessel. We have fully installed the antennas ready for detection, so now hope for updates received to the UPR. If *The Infinity* ceased communication during the Third Global War, then expectations are no message pickup for one year or longer. We will, however, continuously scan for transmission during that time, in the instance a message was sent during the war.

 Would you kindly transmit to us the details of your vessel's system operations to date for analysis?

The UPR wishes all the best for *The Infinity* and once again expresses how pleasing we find your addition to our citizenship alongside *The Eternity*.

All hail the UPR! May the king live long and vigorously!

The UPR have been sending me messages for days and I still don't understand a thing. I scan every word, trying to read the truth behind the messages. Who are the UPR? What's really happening on Earth? They keep sending me robotic messages with a lot of words but not much useful information. The UPR are obsessed with the running of their newly repossessed ships, and not at all interested in telling us what's actually going on back on Earth.

I don't know what to think. I just know that I don't trust them. I can tell J doesn't, either.

Is Molly still working at NASA or for the UPR? Is she even alive? I don't think they are ever going to tell me.

The UPR know that their messages are our only communication with Earth, but they still treat us like computer systems they need to relay orders to. I refuse to send them any information about my ship, at least not until I know that I can definitely trust them.

The ship's system data used to transmit to NASA, but that stopped when the antennas went down. I'm not going to start sending it to the UPR instead. Who knows what they would do with the data? I'm not an idiot.

They have no right to tell J and me what to do. They didn't build these ships. They don't own us.

From: The Eternity   Sent: 05/15/2066
To: The Infinity   Received: 06/09/2067

Romy,

I realized today that I'm in mourning for Earth.

I don't think it's homesickness anymore, because the Earth I was homesick for only exists in my memory. If I went back now, everything would be different. My old home would be unrecognizable.

I don't feel sad about the UPR, I just feel numb. Well, that's not entirely true. I feel angry—and frustrated, the same as I felt after my parents died. Back then, I couldn't focus on anything beyond this wild fury, which made me want to do anything it took to right the wrong of their deaths.

How do you react to grief, Romy? How did you react after your parents died? How did *they* feel after the deaths of the rest of the crew? Did they feel guilty? Did it consume them? Or did they carry on with life as normal?

J x

DAYS UNTIL *THE ETERNITY* ARRIVES:
259

From: The Infinity   Sent: 06/11/2067

To: The Eternity   Predicted date of receipt: 08/15/2067

J,

Firstly, I'm sorry this reply is a couple of days late. It took me a while to write it. I wanted to get it exactly right.

Your reaction seems completely understandable to me. Everyone deals with grief in different ways. Anger is just one of the stages.

After my parents died, I didn't feel sad either—or in denial, or any of the other things you're supposed to feel. I just felt scared. I was too busy trying to work out how to survive each day to take the time to actually grieve. I think I was in shock.

I knew we were isolated out here, but I didn't mind it so much when I had my dad to look after me.

He did everything. He cooked and cleaned and maintained the ship; he educated me and hugged me and loved me and read me bedtime stories. He was my best friend—my only friend. And then all of a sudden, he was gone.

For the first time, I had to do everything he'd done for me by myself. I couldn't accept that I was responsible for it all. Like I told you before, I even tried to turn the ship around.

I curled up in bed and only moved when my bladder hurt so much that I had to use the bathroom, or I had to eat. I didn't even let myself sleep, because whenever I fell asleep I had these awful nightmares where I relived everything that had happened. I just watched *Loch & Ness* over and over.

I was so terrified of my nightmares that I used to pile every piece of furniture that wasn't screwed down in front of my bedroom door. I wasn't taking any chances of someone getting in. I was scared of being alone and scared of *not* being alone, all at once.

That was my whole life, for over two years, until Molly started talking to me and rescued me from myself.

So trust me, however you react to grief, you're doing a better job than me.

My parents are another example of how everyone reacts differently. After the crew died, they were both so upset. I was only young, but I picked up on that—I still have nightmares about the astronauts all the time.

I think it helped my dad that he had to put on a happy face for four-year-old me. He kept up the routine of day-to-day life for my sake. He didn't lose himself in heartache.

But my mother—she didn't go through the stages of grief like he did, and like you're doing. She shut down completely. For the first year, Dad thought that she would get better. But she never did. She got worse.

She stopped speaking to us completely. Then she refused to be in the same room as us. She couldn't so much as look at me. I wish I knew what I did to deserve that. Even now, I feel guilty for whatever I did wrong.

I wasn't scared of her when she was like that. I was just desperate for her attention. I loved her so much. I used to beg her to play with me, to notice me. I used to bring her pictures of animals and plants that I'd copied out for her embroideries, or cookies and cakes I'd attempted to bake. None of it worked.

My dad tried to help. He loved her more than anyone—more than me. He spent years trying everything he could to help her cope with the trauma she'd internalized. He didn't stop trying, not until it was too late. Not until they died because of it.

Just remember, J, you're coping with everything the best way you can, and that's all that matters. Don't ever think you aren't strong.

The UPR makes me feel numb too.

R x

DAYS UNTIL *THE ETERNITY* ARRIVES:
254

From: UPR
To: The Infinity
Subject: For Attention of The Infinity

Sent: 09/30/2065
Received: 06/16/2067

Commander Silvers,

To reiterate our last message, if you have not already done so, please transfer all systems data to Earth for further study. It is of utmost importance we receive this data, as no vessel analytics were picked up by the UPR or NASA during the war.

New data will help us to perform mission analysis and suggest improvements to the operating conditions of *The Infinity*. We also wish to ensure that the background level of radiation and electromagnetic energy are not damaging to health.

Thank you for your cooperation. More instructions for further improvements to arrive in the coming weeks.

All hail the UPR! May the king live long and vigorously!

I had hoped the UPR's last request for information was a casual request, but it wasn't. They're going to keep asking me, over and over, until I break down and agree. They're going to try and interfere with every aspect of my mission. I always knew the people on Earth didn't trust me to do this by myself.

It's not right, what they're doing. They can't take over at the last minute and change everything! I fire off an angry reply, unable to hold my tongue any longer.

I watch the email transmit. Each byte of data explodes inside my chest, spreading painfully through me.

From: The Infinity   Sent: 06/16/2067

To: UPR   Predicted date of receipt: 03/07/2069

Dear Sir/Madam,

I appreciate your attempts to form a peaceful collaboration between the UPR and *The Infinity*. However, I regret to inform you that I am unable to cooperate with your requests at this time.

I do not feel comfortable sending you any information about my ship until I know more about the circumstances involved in your takeover of NASA. The details of the events of the Third Global War in your first message were a little sparse. Could you expand on the situation?

I would also like to know whether an employee of NASA called Dr. Molly Simmons is still working on my mission, after NASA's management changed hands. Did she become a UPR citizen after the UPR took over North America? I would be very grateful if you could tell me anything you know about her current whereabouts and status.

Regards,

Commander Romy Silvers

DAYS UNTIL *THE ETERNITY* ARRIVES:
253

From: The Eternity

To: The Infinity

Sent: 06/09/2066

Received: 06/17/2067

Romy,

When I was little, I never did well in school. I hated my teacher, and I thought the classes were stupid. I just couldn't work in controlled environments—I thrived most when I was left to my own devices.

Before she died, my mom would always tell me that however much I hated my teacher, I needed to do what she said, because she was the boss and I wasn't. She said that I should respect authority, because they had been put in charge for a reason, even if I personally didn't like them.

I think that's the case with the UPR. We might not like them—we might hate everything about them—but they have all the power.

I don't want to feel like I'm living in someone else's world, where there's an external force telling me what to do. But they have all the information, and *I need* to know what has happened to my friends. I'll do anything they ask if it might help persuade them to send us the details about what happened in the war.

We have to choose what we object to very carefully. As long as it doesn't harm us, I think it's best that we agree to their demands. If you can't help the UPR for yourself, then please do it for me. They could cut off all our contact with Earth if they wanted to, and I couldn't handle that. Not when we're already so alone.

Besides, even if I don't trust them at all, I have to admit that they've made some suggestions about my ship's life-support efficiency that have actually been really helpful. I know they're asking you to make some changes to your ship too, which have probably been even more useful, as your ship is so much older. Grudgingly, I must say they know what they're talking about.

I'm sorry. I wish there was something I could do to protect you from this—from them. I feel so powerless. I'm sure you do too.

At least they can't stop us from talking to each other.

J x

From: The Infinity   Sent: 06/17/2067
To: The Eternity   Predicted date of receipt: 08/18/2067

J,

I wish I'd waited to see what you said before replying to the UPR.

My dad always taught me the opposite of your mother. He told me to do whatever I thought was right—like he did, when he and my mother ignored NASA's advice after she got pregnant.

They were supposed to terminate the pregnancy, change shifts with another set of caretakers, and go into torpor sleep. If they had, I would never have been born. Dad stood by their decision to keep me, even after what happened with the astronauts. He used to say that someone outside of a situation is never able to truly judge the best actions to take.

I've always believed that. But I didn't consider you. I didn't think about all the people you know on Earth, about everything you could stand to lose if the UPR cut us off. I'm not the only one who is affected by my actions anymore. I should have thought about the impact this would have on you, instead of just getting angry.

I won't send them any more defensive emails. I'll play nice. I can't promise that I'll do everything the UPR ask, because I still don't trust them. But from now on, if their requests are logical, I'll at least consider it—for you.

I'll send them the information they want. It's a good idea to analyze the background levels of radiation. I admit that is a useful suggestion at least.

R x

There was never supposed to be just one person on *The Infinity*. There was supposed to be a whole population. An entire generation of astronauts trained and prepared for this mission. They were put into a deep-sleep state called "torpor," which was developed for long-duration missions. The astronauts would have remained in the biological hibernation until the ship arrived at the new planet, where they would have woken up without having aged a single day in over forty years.

My parents were the first pair of caretakers. They had volunteered to stay awake on the initial leg of the journey to run the ship and safeguard the sleeping passengers, growing old in the process. They had been trained to live alone on *The Infinity* and make sure everything remained operational.

If everything had gone to plan, after five years they would have woken up another pair of astronauts and left the ship in their care while they went into torpor sleep. But I was born. To say that NASA wasn't pleased is an understatement. My birth meant that my parents had to stay awake instead of swapping places with another pair of astronauts. It messed up the whole plan.

Eventually, NASA accepted it and came up with a new mission timeline. My parents were told to remain as caretakers until I was eighteen, when I would be old enough to enter torpor sleep myself. Then the three of us would have gone into stasis and only woken up again when we arrived on Earth II.

Once that was decided, I became the pride of *The Infinity*: the first child born in space, the start of the new generation, the emblem of all that the mission would achieve.

In the end, all I am is a symbol of its failure.

*** *** ***

I'm keeping track of the number of days until *The Eternity* reaches me, written in whiteboard marker on the plexiglass wall between the kitchen and lounge area.

Two hundred and fifty-three: the number of days I'll have to survive on my own. The number of nights I'll have to worry about running this ship alone. Every hour feels endless and pointless now that I'm just waiting for J.

I decide music will help distract me. I make the computer's controls into an electric keyboard and start practicing my piano chords. I play all of the loudest songs I know, turning the volume up and filling the ship with the sound of music until I don't feel so small and quiet and helpless.

I only stop when my fingers start to ache from playing. Then I turn on some pop music instead, singing along as loudly as I can. I jump down into the lounge area, dancing on the sofa and trying to recapture the carefree happiness I felt when I first started talking to *The Eternity* and everything seemed so hopeful for once.

I make myself dance until I can't ignore the fact that it isn't working, that I just feel worse than ever. I collapse onto the floor, trying to catch my breath. Staring through the porthole, I watch the spiraling stars until I make myself dizzy. I let my vision blur until the constant glow of a distant nebula turns a soft red, then blue, then yellow, then the darkest, deepest green.

DAYS UNTIL *THE ETERNITY* ARRIVES:
249

From: UPR Sent:10/04/2065

To: The Infinity Received: 06/21/2067

Subject: For Attention of The Infinity

Attachment: Linux-Infinity-OS.zip [17 TB]

Commander Silvers,

Judging from evaluations of old NASA data of *The Infinity*, you must change several elements of lifestyle in order to improve energy efficiency and system lifetime extension in all cases.

Over the next twenty-seven hours following this message, we will be transmitting a large program to *The Infinity*. Please install the operating system on your computer. It contains multiple updates to the current Command, Data Handling, and Flight Data subsystems, which are over a decade out of date. It will allow more autonomous control of the vessel's devices, such as improvement of translational and altitude control in the X-ray telescope observatory and the thrust throttling.

This software is used on board *The Eternity*, but NASA felt that it was not worth the cost of transmission from Earth to update the system on *The Infinity* too. However, the UPR has decided it is a worthwhile expense to ensure that any errors in the system are fixed. We do not want any operational failures due to code decay.

Thank you for your cooperation.

All hail the UPR! May the king live long and vigorously!

I've started getting a sick feeling in my stomach every time I open a new email from the UPR. Even though I know that the changes they are suggesting make sense, I still have to fight against my better judgment to agree. My instinct tells me that this latest request is a trick, that they're sending me some kind of virus. If I install it, they might be able to open the airlocks, shut down the life-support system, and leave me to suffocate.

But what possible advantage could they get from sending me software that would damage my ship? From what they've said, getting *The Infinity* and *The Eternity* was a big victory for them in the Third Global War. Why would they destroy the ships now?

J is right. I can't let my emotions get in the way of being a good commander. I'll be hurting *The Infinity* if I don't follow their guidelines to improve the ship.

I've been so convinced that the UPR are the bad guys, that

they only want to hurt me. But I'm going to have to do what they say.

I'll wait and see what the program looks like when it arrives. I know a little about programming. I'll see what updates they've made, and if they really do what they've said.

It'll take twenty-seven hours to receive, anyway. I can change my mind before it arrives.

It's the two-year anniversary of *The Eternity*'s launch today. I wonder if J is celebrating, or if he's regretting ever having left Earth at all.

DAYS UNTIL *THE ETERNITY* ARRIVES:
247

The new operating system has finished uploading, and I still haven't decided whether I'm going to install it. Something just doesn't feel right. I can't tell if my anxiety is my usual paranoia, or whether this is actually something worth worrying about.

I wish I could talk to J about this, in real time. He doesn't seem to know that the UPR have told me to upgrade my OS to match the one he uses on *The Eternity*—or, at least, he didn't mention it in his last email. There's no reason why they would need to tell him, I suppose.

It's not like I can ask his opinion on what to do, either—it would be two months before he even received my message. I'm going to have to make this decision on my own.

Even if the UPR are genuinely trying to help me, surely there's a chance they've missed something? What if the new program has a mistake in the coding that accidentally shuts down something vital on the ship?

Decades ago, a spacecraft crash-landed on Mars because NASA messed up the units in their calculations. Half the team were using inches and the rest centimeters. The trajectory went completely off course and the spacecraft disintegrated in the atmosphere.

What if the UPR use a different set of units from the ones NASA used? What if I install their program and *The Infinity* sets off to a different area of space, and I never get to Earth II? What if it alters the rotation of the ship and sends the gravity haywire, making the ship spin faster and faster until the centrifugal force pushes my brain through my spinal column like soup?

There are so many reasons to ignore their suggestion—but there are *always* reasons for me to hide under my duvet and do nothing instead of acting. I need to start taking more risks.

If anything goes wrong, I have to believe that I will be able to fix it. There's no reason why I shouldn't be able to handle any problems that come up. And it'll be worth it, if it makes the ship more efficient.

The UPR haven't lied to me yet. J thinks I should listen to them, and he's got more reason to dislike them than anyone, seeing as they took control of his country.

I'm going to do it. I'm going to install the program.

Holding my breath, I click on the file and watch the loading bar crawl across the screen. Have I just made a huge mistake, or have I added another decade to the lifetime of the ship?

I guess I'll find out in thirty hours, when the program has finished installing.

I wake up in the middle of the night to an email telling me that the UPR have decided to end my mission. They've cut *The Infinity*'s power. There's nothing I can do about it.

The lights stay on for an hour, then slowly, one by one, start to flicker out. I follow the last traces of power from room to room, until at last I'm in the gene bank, surrounded by floating cells in liquid.

Then the final light goes out, and I'm alone in the dark

forever

they're moving

eyes opening

staring at me in the darkness

and I can't see

but I can hear them

murmuring

I can feel their fingers touching my face

tangling in my hair

their soft fingernails

skin pulling away from their bones

catching on my clothes

the embryos are falling apart around me

silently reaching for their mother

wanting me
and I'm alone
in the dark
forever

I wake up gasping for breath.

I swear the shadows move. They lunge across the floor every time I look away, casting the shape of their long bodies around the ship's walls. All I can do is lie in bed under the weight of their stares, their eyes lingering on me in the corner of my vision.

The dark, blunted shadows hold me under the duvet where the childlike safe place in my brain says they can't find me. The shadows dart and swell across the room and all I can do is watch them creep closer.

DAYS UNTIL *THE ETERNITY* ARRIVES:
245

When I check the helm in the morning, the computer's home screen welcomes me in a glowing, almost-fluorescent blue. The words "Hello, Romy" scroll across the screen and smoothly disappear. My inbox opens without me having to do anything, displaying J's latest email.

I grin, already convinced that this was a good idea after all. It looks fresh and modern, and—in comparison with the old program—almost unbelievably advanced. In an emergency, it's going to be able to react so much faster. It could end up saving my life.

For the first time, I feel slightly relieved that the UPR are messaging me. Even if it's not NASA, it's nice to know that there's someone looking out for me.

J,

I have some bad news. The UPR updated the software on my ship's computer, and the new program has a censoring subroutine. I can't swear in my emails anymore—look: **** ******* ***** **** ****

It's ****ing terrible!

Just kidding. When I swore for you before, that was literally the only time I ever have, I think. I'm not sure I'd even know which finger to stick up!

I don't mind the censoring—and the new program is actually great. It's the same one you have on *The Eternity*. The previous version was *nineteen years old*, so this one is ridiculously good in comparison.

My favorite parts are the little logic puzzles, and the way I can project things on the walls of the ship.

I still don't trust the UPR—not until I make sure that Molly is OK, at least. But I'd be stupid to let my emotions stop me from taking advantage of the gift they've given me.

I hope you're holding up OK. I hope that by the time you're reading this, the UPR have finally told you where all of your friends are.

R x

DAYS UNTIL *THE ETERNITY* ARRIVES:
233

From: The Eternity   Sent: 08/12/2066

To: The Infinity   Received: 07/07/2067

Hey, Romy,

All I've been thinking about recently is the UPR. I feel tied up in knots about them.

I can hardly bear to think about what the war has done to my home.

Right now I just want to find some peace. I feel scattered in a million different directions, trying to make sure I'm good enough to do my job properly, trying to work out how to deal with the UPR—not just for myself but for you too.

I don't want to give you bad advice. I know you're probably going through exactly the same thing as me. Don't you give up on me, Romy, not yet. I'm coming—just hold on a little longer. It will be easier when we're together.

Urgh. It's messing me up, talking about this. I don't want every message I send you to be just about the UPR. I'd hate to stop having proper conversations because of them.

J x

DAYS UNTIL *THE ETERNITY* ARRIVES:
227

I wake up to an emergency alarm blaring from the computer. A memory of my mother flashes across my mind: her kneeling down to look me in the eye when I was just a toddler.

"Now, Romy," she said. "What do you do if you hear the emergency alarms?"

"Find you and Daddy?" I said.

She shook her head. "No. You find the nearest oxygen mask. You put it on, and wait for us to find you. Don't do anything until you've got your mask on."

Remembering her words, I reach under my bunk, opening the panel that contains an oxygen mask. I pull it on, breathing in deeply, and tug the canister over my shoulder. I run to the helm to read the message on the new UPR software, already panicking.

SYSTEM FAILURE IN EMBRYO STORAGE SYSTEM 12(c)

AUTO-DEFROST WILL COMMENCE IN 5 . . . 4 . . . 3 . . .

The freezers in the gene bank have crashed. If I don't do something, the embryos are going to start defrosting. They'll be destroyed.

Barely breathing, I run down the corridor to the gene bank and reboot the system. The computer slowly powers back up. Every second it takes to load, the warmer the embryos get. I urge it to go faster.

An eternity later, the system comes back online and the error message has gone away. I scan the subsystem for issues, but it comes back clean. I think—I hope—that the problem has been fixed.

The embryos might have been destroyed. Hundreds of potential lives could have been lost.

Pacing back and forth down the corridor, I try to process how this could have happened. This is making me wonder whether there have been failures happening in hardware all over the ship. I need to start running analysis tests. Now.

DAYS UNTIL *THE ETERNITY* ARRIVES:
221

From: The Infinity

To: The Eternity

Sent: 07/19/2067

Predicted date of receipt: 09/08/2067

J,

I have done nothing productive today, just worried about the ship, and about the war, and about staying alive long enough to reach the new planet, and about every other thing I can come up with.

I've had some issues with the ship recently—equipment crashing, computers malfunctioning, that sort of thing. I can't tell whether it's because the new software has a few operating bugs while it settles in or whether it's just because the ship is so old. I don't know which I would prefer.

I can barely sleep anymore, because as soon as I go to bed, my brain decides it needs to sort through every single issue the ship has had in all the time I've been alone and go over them in endless detail until it's six a.m. and all I've done for the last eight hours is stare at the ceiling and panic over things that happened five years ago. It's great.

I hope you're coping a little better now than you were when you sent your last messages. I'm thinking of you.

R x

DAYS UNTIL *THE ETERNITY* ARRIVES:
203

The new software thinks that something needs replacing in the air-conditioning units. It has a much finer sensitivity than the old software, and it thinks there's been a 0.5 percent decrease in efficiency of oxygen recycling over the last quarter. If something is broken, then we could run out of oxygen before we reach Earth II.

Even though I know it's urgent, I don't want to do it. The air-conditioning units are in the room next to the sick bay. Just the thought of going there makes me dizzy. I've avoided that area of the ship for years.

But the computer tells me that I need to.

I wonder if it can wait until J gets here so he can do it for me. He's not that far away, after all. We'd only lose a few weeks' worth of recycled oxygen in that time. But that might be a few weeks' breathing time that we'll desperately need one day.

I walk down the corridor toward the air-conditioning room, pressed against the opposite wall, as far away from the entrance to the sick bay as I can get.

As I approach it, I can't stop myself from breaking into a run. I catch a blurred glimpse of the door as I sprint past, just enough to see that it's still half open, the way it was left all those years ago.

I slam my fist against the button to open the door of the air-conditioning room, keeping my eyes fixed firmly ahead. It seems to slide open far more slowly than any of the other doors. Diving inside, I lean against the wall and gasp for breath. I made it.

As soon as I start paying attention, my relief disappears abruptly. Because I can hear movement.

There's something in the room with me.

Whatever is causing the air-conditioners to lose efficiency is moving. I can hear a low grinding below the quiet hum of the fans, subtle enough that I almost think I'm imagining it.

I brush the thought away and take a step toward the fans. But before my foot hits the floor, every single light shuts off, leaving me in pitch-blackness.

Every muscle in my body freezes.

I can't breathe. I can't think.

I can't be here, not now, not in a power cut.

My mind immediately goes to the sick bay, to the torpor pods, to the astronauts, and a scream bursts from my throat, shrill and short. I throw myself backward against the wall, jarring my shoulder.

But pressed against the safety of the wall, I can focus. I can almost imagine I'd be able to see anything that tries to lunge at me from the darkness.

My mouth tastes of vomit. There are glowing remnants of light darting across my eyelids in the blackness.

Why did the power cut have to happen *now*, when I'm so near the sick bay?

I'm sure I can hear someone coming. The low grinding sound has shifted into the echo of footsteps, progressing down the corridor in a steady, unhurried march. An army of astronauts, coming for me.

Why aren't the lights coming back on? How long does it take for the computer to reboot the subsystem, to—

As suddenly as they flickered off, the lights return. I twist around, checking all sides.

I'm completely alone. Of course.

I breathe again, for the first time in what feels like hours. There's a horrible tightness in my chest, halfway to a panic attack. I force it away, blowing air into my lungs.

I'm being ridiculous. It was just a power cut. It only lasted a few seconds.

Everything in me wants to bolt, but I force myself to stay still. I won't let this hysterical fear get the better of me.

I listen. I wait.

There it is. The creaking. I *didn't* imagine it.

I turn my head from side to side, trying to locate the sound. I take a step closer to the fans on the far wall. There—on the right-hand side, low, near the ground.

I crouch. I listen.

The noise is coming from inside the panel. Before I open it, I can't resist looking behind me, just to double-check that nothing is sneaking up on me. Even though I know I'm alone; I'm always alone.

I ease open the panel, wincing at the high-pitched squeak.

To my relief—and a slight, surprising disappointment—the problem is obvious. One of the screws holding the cooling fan in place has come loose, and the corner of the fan is vibrating slightly as it turns. Its low humming noise echoes through the room.

I twist it back into place. The humming stops. Silence reigns once more. And I start preparing myself to walk back past the sick bay.

DAYS UNTIL *THE ETERNITY* ARRIVES:
172

From: The Eternity   Sent: 02/19/2067
To: The Infinity   Received: 09/06/2067
Attachment: Nuclear-Worksheet-134.pdf [330 KB]

Good morning, Romy!

What are you up to today? I'm planning to do some weight train-ing, and then I'm going to lounge around eating snacks for the rest of the day, and undo all my hard work.

I was wondering if I could ask your help with a physics problem? I know, I know: I'm qualified in all this stuff, so it should be easy. But I've lost practice so quickly! It's been over two years since my training on Earth. No wonder I'm supposed to do regular calcu-lations. My brain needs a workout as much as my body—and right now it's definitely out of shape.

I'm a bit stuck with Problem 6(a) on the worksheet I've

attached. The solution doesn't make much sense to me. Any chance you know the answer and can help me out? I'd really owe you one.

Looking forward to receiving the answer (in about eight months' time!).

J x

From: The Infinity   Sent: 09/06/2067
To: The Eternity   Predicted date of receipt: 10/09/2067
Attachment: Possible-solution.pdf [280 KB]

J,

I've spent about two hours trying to solve the problem. It's one I hadn't seen before, so thanks for sending it over! (I found that way more exciting than I should've. Whoo, someone sent me some new math to do!)

Anyway, I think you might have forgotten to take into account the limits on the partial integration. But you've got most of the rest of it right. I've attached my notes just in case you're still stuck, though you probably realized your mistake right after you emailed me.

Sorry for my terrible handwriting—it's not as neat as yours. (I loved the little doodles in the margin, by the way! Are those people supposed to be us? We look like we're having the best dance party ever.)

Thanks again for asking me about this. It was actually kind of an epiphany for me. I've been struggling to do physics problems for years—it was like my anxiety formed a block in my brain. When I was doing this one, I kept panicking and wanting to give up as usual. But I knew that I had to work it out for you, so I just forced myself to keep going.

Hopefully that mental block won't reappear. I hated that my brain was stopping me from studying.

R x

FATED

by TheLoneliestGirl

Fandom: Loch & Ness (2042)
Relationship: Lyra Loch/Jayden Ness
Tags: NSFW
Summary: Some people are just destined to be together.

Author's note:

I'm having a really good day.

Lyra and Jayden didn't stop to talk. Jayden palmed her jaw and pressed his lips to hers, openmouthed, pouring all of his emotion into it. Lyra shuddered, and reached one hand to cup his elbow, pressing his hand more firmly against her cheek.

Groaning into the kiss, J slid his other hand up her waist, fingertips just touching the skin under her shirt.

She touched the cut of his hip, pulled him against her, flicked his tongue with hers, and suddenly the kiss turned heated. She let out a moan.

J's hand withdrew slowly enough to send sparks down her spine.

"I've been waiting for this moment for so long," Jayden said, nose pressed into her cheekbone. "I haven't been able to think about anything but speaking to you."

He kissed her again, like he couldn't help it.

fin.

DAYS UNTIL *THE ETERNITY* ARRIVES:
171

When I've finished writing my latest fic, I reread the story to check for grammar and spelling mistakes. It's only on the third reread that I notice I wrote J instead of Jayden halfway through: *Groaning into the kiss, J slid his other hand up her waist, fingertips just touching the skin under her shirt.*

Now that I've seen it written down, I can't help but picture J instead of Jayden—but he's kissing me, not Lyra. The image burns into my brain, and I can't force it away. For a second I think my heart has stopped, and I can't remember how to set it beating again. I've gone hot all over.

J and me, kissing. His hand brushing along my stomach, up to my chest . . . I trace the path of his fingers with my own, and my skin lights up, shivers creeping across the flesh, making me gasp.

J works out. He's probably strong enough to push me up

against a wall, his large hand easily cupping my cheek, his thumb pressing open my mouth. He would touch my bottom lip with just the tip of his tongue and stroke it across the sensitive inner skin, teasing me like the men in romance novels always do to the women they love.

I close my eyes and picture J pushing a leg between mine. I press the base of my palm between my legs, savoring the thrill that runs through me. Then I quickly pull my hand away. I can't do this—not to J. Not to the only friend I've got. I don't know how it never occurred to me before, considering I spend every waking hour thinking about him, but . . . I might have a crush on J.

I've set myself up for heartbreak—but I didn't even know it was happening. I thought I was just happy to have a friend, someone to talk to after everyone on Earth abandoned me. I didn't realize that I could feel this *lust* for someone I've never even seen.

I wonder what to do now that I know. Because already I can see that there's no going back.

DAYS UNTIL *THE ETERNITY* ARRIVES:
162

From: UPR
To: The Infinity
Subject: For Attention of The Infinity

Sent: 12/22/2065
Received: 09/16/2067

Commander Silvers,

Analysis of efficiency of the vessel *The Infinity* continues. Once new software is running smoothly, please limit water use by 10 percent. Reducing of shower duration by one minute each day will increase resource utilization and minimize energy loss. It will ensure that equipment is operating at its highest power mode for the full duration of *The Infinity*'s voyage.

Thank you for all your patience while new orders are being determined. More instructions to arrive in the coming weeks.

All hail the UPR! May the king live long and vigorously!

✳✳✳

The ingenious methods that the UPR come up with to save more energy always take me by surprise. They're so obvious that it makes me feel guilty for not thinking of them myself.

The computer failures around the ship have been getting more and more frequent. The lights seem to go off every other day now, even though I've checked everything for faults and found nothing. I've started carrying a flashlight wherever I go.

I don't know whether a power shortage or a fault in the circuits and software is causing the computer failures, but I can't risk doing something that might shut down the freezers or lights again—or, worse, the life-support systems. If that happened, I would probably be dead before I even noticed.

It makes sense to conserve power like the UPR are suggesting, even if efficiency isn't the root of the problem. I have to do it. There's not a doubt in my mind about that. The UPR have been right about everything else so far.

From: The Eternity   Sent: 03/22/2067
To: The Infinity   Received: 09/16/2067

Romy,

I've been thinking about "Earth food" a lot today. It's not that I don't love exploring the universe, but there's a lot of struggles that come with it. One of them is definitely the messed-up cuisine.

I know you've never had real food, just this terrible dehydrated stuff, but I have. I miss it more than I ever thought I could.

I would give almost anything for: pizza, so hot it burns your tongue; a Big Mac with melty plastic cheese and mayonnaise; a bucket of KFC, chicken skin crisped to perfection; a burrito, spilling guacamole and tomato salsa.

But I'm never going to have any of those again, so I guess I'll just have to make do with today's meal, which is apparently . . . solid oxtail soup. It's a real challenge.

From (a very hungry and very frustrated),

J x

From: The Infinity Sent: 09/16/2067
To: The Eternity Predicted date of receipt: 10/16/2067

J,

I'm sorry that spaceship cuisine isn't to your taste. When you arrive, I'll bake chocolate gateau à la Romy. It will make your taste buds explode in delight. (Don't get too excited. It's a recipe I concocted when I was nine, and it's composed mainly of chocolate pudding. There aren't any baking ingredients here either.)

R x

The things I tell J are bigger than I ever intend them to be. My words betray me. With every email I'm making myself vulnerable, showing him how much he means to me.

Ever since I realized how I really feel about him, I've become obsessed. I literally can't stop thinking about us. The idea that we are going to raise the next generation of humans sends electricity tingling down my spine. We're going to be the Adam and Eve of the new planet. It's the most romantic thing I've ever heard. When I think of J, I think: *soul mate* and *forever* and *mine*.

DAYS UNTIL *THE ETERNITY* ARRIVES:
156

I'm chewing on a particularly tough piece of beef in black bean sauce when I feel a sharp twinge in my jaw. I spit the meat into my palm and rub my thumb over the tooth. Pain shoots through my gum, so painful it makes me tear up.

I've been noticing for a while that the tooth aches whenever I drink cold water, but I've been ignoring it, in the hope that it will go away on its own. I don't think it's going to, though.

There's an orthodontic machine on board that performs dental surgery and checkups—you just stick your mouth inside and it does everything itself—but I haven't used it in years. It's in the sick bay. I'd rather put up with any kind of pain than go in there.

I abandon the beef in black bean sauce and eat some porridge instead, carefully pushing it over to the left side of my mouth so that it doesn't touch my aching tooth. I can live with this. It'll be fine.

It *really hurts.*

DAYS UNTIL *THE ETERNITY* ARRIVES:
146

From: The Eternity   Sent: 05/11/2067

To: The Infinity   Received: 10/02/2067

I decided when I woke up that this is not gonna be one of those days where I sit around watching TV. I am going to do something productive. So I've been practicing the flight protocols all day.

The simulation for landing on the new planet is basically a video game, isn't it? In my version, there are little graphics of you and me who jump up and down when the ships touch the ground. Every time I see it, I find it increasingly hard to believe that one day it will really be us. It already feels like I've been traveling forever.

J xx

On my run today, I came up with an idea for using the UPR's new software to make my route more interesting. I can project other runners on the walls of the corridor and race them around the ship.

I look through the archives on the hard drive, and track down some old Wii Fit video games with running scenes. I add two new avatars to the game so that it looks like I'm racing Jayden and Lyra.

To my delight, it actually works.

I let Jayden win, just so I can stand, sweaty and panting for breath, and watch the avatar lift up his arms. He celebrates his victory with a silly dance, fireworks filling the screen behind him.

I'm overwhelmed with sudden gratitude to the UPR for giving me something so lovely. With their new software, it's like they've actually *sent me Jayden Ness*. A life-size model of him!

I press my hand against the wall, standing so close that his grinning face is just a blur of pixels, and wish with every atom of my body that this wasn't just a simulation; that Jayden was really here with me.

I keep thinking about what it will be like when the ships finally meet. J and I will hug, wrapping ourselves up in each other for endless seconds. In my head, he smells of lime and wood. He'll brush the hair away from my face, and his thumb will move in slow sweeps across the back of my hand.

I want that to come true. Soon.

I can't believe that I get to talk to J every day. I can't believe he's as excited to meet me as I am to meet him; that he pictures us together on Earth II.

Today he put two kisses at the end of his email. We've come such a long way from when we called each other Commander Silvers and Commander Shoreditch.

DAYS UNTIL *THE ETERNITY* ARRIVES:
144

From: UPR
To: The Infinity
Subject: For Attention of The Infinity

Sent: 01/07/2066
Received: 10/04/2067

Commander Silvers,

Hoping all is well on *The Infinity* and no problem is occurring with any system. We write today to ask that, as a follow-up to water conservation, you reduce shower time by half to increase efficiency and also reduce toilet flushing unless necessary.

This will save on chemical processing of sewage water as well as electrical heat production.

Thank you for your cooperation.

All hail the UPR! May the king live long and vigorously!

I know the UPR mean well with their efficiency suggestions, but it's already hard enough to reduce my showers by just one minute. I have to turn off the water while I shampoo my hair and lather up the soap, then turn it back on again to rinse off. I can't imagine being able to get properly clean in half that time.

The UPR are right, though. I shouldn't take my privileges for granted.

This all seems logical. Despite that, there's a blossoming concern in my mind, as always. There's no reason for me to panic over these helpful suggestions, but my brain doesn't seem to want to listen.

It's probably just because my tooth still hurts. It's becoming more and more painful. There's now a continuous sharp pain along my jaw. Whenever I roll over in my sleep, I wake up from the pressure of the pillow.

I've checked the ship's inventory and there isn't a spare orthodontics kit in the stores. The sick bay is my only option. But just the thought of going inside the room makes tears spring to my eyes.

I take some antibiotics from the first-aid kit in the living area instead, hoping that will be enough to kill whatever infection is causing the pain.

DAYS UNTIL *THE ETERNITY* ARRIVES:
141

The antibiotics haven't made any difference to my toothache. If anything, it's worse. It hurts so much that I can't think about anything else.

I know it's my own fault for letting my teeth get so bad. I've been ignoring the computer's six-monthly dental checkup reminders for years, trying to avoid going into the sick bay. These days I barely even remember to floss. I deserve this pain.

I shine a flashlight into my mouth, staring at the painful tooth using a handheld mirror. The molar is a brownish-black color. It's completely rotten through.

Feeling slightly nauseated, I compare my tooth to pictures of cavities in the medical subprogram. Judging by the photographs, it's too late to fix it with a filling. It needs to be extracted.

I'm going to have to remove one of my teeth.

I just wish that I could do it somewhere apart from the sick bay. The manual tells me that the orthodontic equipment there can remove the tooth without me having to do anything but open my mouth—and there's a topical anesthetic, so I wouldn't feel a thing. It sounds easy. It sounds quick. But I know I'm not going to do this the easy way.

I can picture exactly what's waiting inside the sick bay and there's no way I can go in there. I'm going to remove this tooth old-school style. People have been extracting teeth for millennia without fancy space-age NASA technology. I don't need machinery to do this—I just need some pliers.

I read through the manual's instructions on tooth extraction, making a list of essentials. I can create dentistry tools from cutlery and sewing supplies. Just as long as I don't have to go into the sick bay, anything will do.

I find a scalpel, a screwdriver, and a set of pliers in the maintenance tool kit. There's a medium-strength anesthetic and bandages in the first-aid kit. I fetch a tea towel from the kitchen, just in case there's more blood than in the pictures in the manual. I also take the few centimeters of whiskey left at the bottom of Dad's bottle.

After sterilizing the equipment with boiling water, I prepare a clean area of the bathroom for surgery and change into an old pair of coveralls. I rub a capsule of anesthetic on my gum, and while I wait for it to work I read through the instructions for the seventh time.

When the pain in my jaw has weakened noticeably, I have no other choice but to start.

I pick up the pliers. A dizzy feeling passes through me. I ignore it. I am a strong, independent woman and I can totally do this.

Thinking carefully about anything other than what I'm about to do, I touch the pliers against either side of the rotten tooth. When I press down, a searing pain shoots up my jaw. I drop the pliers, gasping. The tool skitters across the floor, coming to a stop at the base of the toilet.

OK. So, maybe some more painkillers are needed. And another round of sterilization.

Four hours later, there are fragments of tooth, gum, and blood all over the sink. My tongue feels dry and thick, pressed against the padding where my tooth used to be. But the tooth is out, and my jaw is numb.

There were a few moments when I almost resigned myself to living with a wobbly, rotten tooth hanging halfway out of my mouth forever. But I pushed through, knowing that if I gave up I'd never pluck up the courage to try again.

Eventually I managed to lever the tooth out with the screwdriver in only three fragments. I call that a success. I promise myself that I will floss twice a day, every single day, from now on. I am *never* doing that again.

Ignoring the post-surgery mess, I stagger to my bunk and fall headfirst into it. I've spent so long running on pure adrenaline that I'm exhausted.

I'm sure tomorrow my whole face will be covered in bruises, but for now I just want to sleep.

DAYS UNTIL *THE ETERNITY* ARRIVES:
136

From: UPR   Sent: 01/14/2066
To: The Infinity   Received: 10/12/2067
Subject: For Attention of The Infinity

Commander Silvers,

Following previous communications to undertake improvements to *The Infinity*, we have more requests for lifestyle changes.

To help the vessel survive voyage in maximum condition, we require you to reduce hours of light usage. Please limit effective "daylight" hours to 90 percent parts of current usage hours. This will allow better energy efficiency.

Thank you for your cooperation.

All hail the UPR! May the king live long and vigorously!

After I read the UPR's latest email, I open up the landing simulator and fly the ship aimlessly around the planet.

Cutting down to 90 percent of the daylight hours means there will be nearly two extra hours of darkness a day. I suppose it won't be that bad. I can just go to bed an hour earlier, and have a longer lie-in in the mornings.

On the simulation, orange flames lick the hull as *The Infinity* passes through the atmosphere.

It's definitely worth turning out the lights earlier in the day if it means there won't be any more power cuts. I've gotten used to the lights going out at random times, but it's still irritating—especially if I'm in the middle of a run, when it messes up my timings.

As the ship glides down toward a burnt-orange desert in the simulation, dust lifting up to greet it, I'm filled with the sudden urge to push down hard on the accelerator. I watch *The Infinity* crash into the surface of the planet. It explodes in flames, metal shards flying in all directions. The destruction makes me feel satisfied in a way I know it shouldn't.

I restart the simulation and crash the ship into the ground again, watching the tiny model people drown in ice-coated oceans and crumple under avalanches on volcanoes. My score keeps dropping until I'm at the lowest level, where I don't have enough control to crash the ship.

Now I can't even do what I want on a *computer game*. And my gum is still so sore that I can't eat without jarring it.

I hate everything.

DAYS UNTIL *THE ETERNITY* ARRIVES:
131

According to the software's diagnosis of the maintenance system, there's a slight blockage in one of the air ventilation panels. The computer tells me that I need to remove it before it begins to affect maximum performance.

The schematic of the vents looks like a cobweb of tunnels, covering every meter of the ship. A blockage glows red on the diagram, somewhere forty meters above the gene bank in the stores. That's . . . really high up. It's closer to the center of the ship than I've ever been before. I'll be venturing up into the dark core of *The Infinity*. It has hardly been visited since the ship was built.

The supplies are stored in the center of the ship, where the hubcap of a wheel would be. There are ladders every ten meters or so along the corridor, a bit like the spokes on a wheel. They lead up into different parts of the stores, although it's all connected up there. Apart from fuel, it's nearly all food. There had to be enough supplies to support several humans for most of their lives, after all. That doesn't leave much room for anything besides freeze-dried produce and medicine. But as there's just me here now, the food supplies have barely been touched at this point in the journey. It's crammed up there.

Sometimes I get cravings for things so badly that I waste an entire day moving boxes to search through the vacuum-packed food in search of tomato soup or chocolate. You can crawl around the whole of the stores if you're small enough to get between the boxes.

I grab my headlamp and a bottle of water, and head to the access ladder outside the lounge area, which leads up to the miscellaneous section of the stores. The trapdoor in the ceiling opens easily when I tug at it, and I use my headlight to shine a light up the shaft. It's a square tunnel only just wider than my shoulders. It curves gently upward, until the passage disappears out of sight and my flashlight beam turns into flickering shadows.

I count each rung as I climb up, looking down at the glow of light from the lounge area disappearing out of sight below me. The gravity in the center of the ship is weaker than on the ground level, because it's created using rotational force. I feel my body lighten as I climb. If it wasn't so tightly packed, the food would float in midair like old-fashioned astronauts used to.

The shaft of the ladder opens up into a grid of shelves, stacked tightly with supplies. Gaps between the stacks form paths, most of which Dad carved out when the ship first launched.

I find myself relaxing as I climb. It's reassuring up here, enclosed on every side. Protected. I know nothing is coming. I would hear it, knocking over boxes and scattering food packets.

If the astronauts ever did come back for me, they would never be able to find me up here. That makes me feel safe, even if the ghosts are just a figment of my imagination.

Once, I found a whole section of farming equipment, with tools and machinery ready to be used on Earth II. There's even an all-terrain exploration vehicle. I used to crawl into its cabin when I wanted somewhere private to sulk.

Above me, I catch sight of something written on the side of a box. I climb faster to get to it, and shine my light on thick black lines of permanent marker. It's not writing—it's a wobbly doodle by a young child. I must have come up here to draw when I was little. I would have been very young, though, because I don't remember it at all.

There are three stick figures standing in a line, holding hands. They're on top of a roughly drawn circle, which I think is supposed to be the ship—or maybe it's a planet.

One of the figures is a lot shorter than the others, with a big semicircle of a beaming smile. It's supposed to be me, I realize.

The drawing is of me and Dad and my mother. The bottom drops out of my stomach.

In the picture, she's smiling too.

I turn the box around so I can't see the drawing, and carry on moving.

After thirty rungs, I can feel the ache in my limbs. I make a mental note to do more weight training. The map on my tablet starts flashing, showing me the route to the blocked ventilation panel. I need to crawl into a narrow horizontal shaft between the stacks. Dad used to make me climb into gaps like these on the lower levels to fetch supplies, when I was small enough to slide between the boxes.

My size allowed me to hide up here once. It saved my life.

I push away the thought. I'm not supposed to let myself think about that time, not here, where it might trigger a panic attack.

I lever myself into the tunnel. It's a tight fit, with barely any room to move my limbs, and the metal is smooth and slippery.

It occurs to me as I shuffle forward that I won't be able to stop myself from sliding headfirst if the shaft curves back downward. But it's too late now—there isn't enough space to turn around. I have to keep going. Already I'm struggling to keep track of where I am in the ship.

My knuckles hit the lower rungs of a ladder. The map is still flashing, so I start climbing upward again.

I'm halfway up the shaft when I notice that it's suddenly a

lot easier to climb. Effortless, in fact. I grab on to the rungs with both hands, staring down at my legs where they dangle in midair.

I'm *floating*. I'm floating!

I must have reached the very center of the stores. Up here, in the middle of the ship, the force of the artificial gravity is lower. I can float like a real astronaut on a space station.

I kick my feet, watching them swing around in nothing, and let out a happy laugh. Pushing gently against the wall with one finger, I drift up the tunnel as easily as breathing.

As my hair twists up around my head, I delight in the way that just the smallest touch can send me flying off in another direction.

When my tablet lets out a beep in my pocket I pull myself to a stop. I must be close to the blockage. I orient myself with the map. The obstruction is apparently just above me.

The panel looks normal, but maybe the blockage is on the other side. I open it and shine my headlight inside. I'm expecting to see rows of boxes, but instead there are stacks of neatly folded fabric.

One of the stacks has collapsed and the material floats in midair, clumping against the panel's opening. Presumably it set off the computer's sensors.

I'm overwhelmed by the amount of fabric here. It has never occurred to me to track down the fabric supplies on the ship before. There are boxes of ready-made clothes in different sizes in the lower levels of the stores, but it's all in the uni-sex, functional style of NASA uniforms. Most of the time that means *coveralls*. With uncut fabric, I could design and make my own clothes completely from scratch. Pretty things, like dresses and skirts and cardigans—and scarves!

My mother was always sewing. It was one of the things she liked doing best, after the astronauts. She would disappear into a small corner in the back of the sick bay, and reappear days later with an intricate piece of embroidery she'd created on an old blanket or towel.

When Dad and I would coo over them, she'd hand them to us, already picking up more material. The embroideries used to hang on the walls of the corridor, their bright colors and abstract designs lighting up the gray walls. I tore them all down when my parents died and put them in the organic waste disposal. I wish I hadn't, now that the anger has dulled a little. They were beautiful. There's nothing on the walls any-more except the crayon drawings I used to do as a child.

Sometimes, if I begged my mother and she was feeling really good, she would show me how to thread a needle or tie a knot. But after only a few minutes she would just freeze, and this horrible expression would come over her face when she looked at me. Then she'd disappear into the sick bay again, and we'd go back to only seeing her when we brought her food.

I could never understand what I did wrong. What was it

about me that stopped her from loving me the way Dad did? I think I must have been too loud, too energetic for her.

Hovering in place, I pull the sheaths of fabric into the tunnel, clearing the obstruction. I'm definitely taking some of it back with me.

I see a shining mustard-yellow fabric and add that to my pile, already planning the outfits I can make. I can't resist choosing a beautiful pale purple fabric and a vivid dark green one as well.

Wrapping the material around my shoulders, I memorize the other colors I can see, so I can plan what to take next time.

For now, I think I should go back to the living quarters. I'm feeling a bit . . . tired. There are tiny little bumps all over my arms and I feel kind of shivery, especially in my lower back.

By the time I reach ground level, my lips and fingertips are slightly numb. Maybe I'm getting ill? When I give a full-body shudder, the sensation reminds me of an animal from a cartoon, shivering in the snow. I'm *cold*, I realize, surprised.

The lumps on my arms must be goose bumps. I run my fingers over them, amazed that my body has been able to do something so strange all this time, without me knowing about it.

I've never been cold before. The climate on the ship is always set at a comfortable room temperature.

I wrap myself in a blanket, trying to work out why I'm suddenly freezing. Has the temperature of the ship dropped somehow?

At the helm, there's another error message on the screen. It's hours' old:

POWER FAILURE IN HEATER 43(f)

The heating system must have crashed and shut down while I was in the stores. No wonder I'm shivering—the temperature of the ship has lowered by six degrees. I'm lucky that only one of the heater quadrants failed. If all of the ship's temperature regulators had shut down, I would have died, frozen in my tunnel as the heat leaked out into space and the temperature dropped below zero.

I reboot the heater, wrapping myself in more blankets while it begins working in overdrive to raise the temperature again.

I attempt to start analyzing the system data to isolate what exactly went wrong, but I end up staring blankly at the screen, lost in thought. The letters blur and double before my eyes.

I don't understand why there have been so many system failures so long after the new software was installed. It's natural for a new OS to have a few bugs, but this is ridiculous. First the embryo freezers, then the air-conditioning and lighting, and now the heating.

I have no idea what to do about it. I've tried every troubleshooting solution I can think of, but I still can't work out where all the shortages are coming from. Even though I've asked the UPR and J for advice, by the time they work out what the problem is and send me the solution, it'll be far too late.

Maybe it's time for me to accept that this ship is old now. That it's falling apart around me.

I just have to hope that *The Eternity* gets here before *The Infinity* breaks down permanently. All I can do until then is keep saving as much power as possible to try and make sure the ship lasts that long.

Once J is here, all my problems will disappear. I just have to hold on.

DAYS UNTIL *THE ETERNITY* ARRIVES:
125

From: The Eternity

To: The Infinity

Sent: 07/16/2067

Received: 10/23/2067

Romy,

Sometimes I feel like you're the only thing in my life that I can depend on. Everything around me is in a constant flux of uncertainty, except for you. You're always there for me. *The Eternity* is a beaut, but it doesn't feel like home to me. *You* do. And I feel that way even though I've only ever emailed you! Imagine how I'll feel when we're spending every day together.

I'm so psyched to meet you in person. It's better talking to you now that we're sending messages back and forth with less of a delay. It's more of a conversation now that I get your reply after only a few weeks.

I think that the first time we meet we'll have to sit down and just tell each other things for three days straight. I usually end up cutting out half of what I've written in these emails, because they get so long. I can't help it. I never mean to, but as soon as I start writing, it turns out I have so much to tell you.

I guess what I'm trying to say is that I really like you, Romy. More than I expected to. To be honest, I was really nervous about getting in touch—I had no idea what you would be like. Now I can't wait to see you.

I wonder if we would have been friends if we had been meeting in less exceptional circumstances. I hope so. I really do, neighbor.

J xx

J likes me! Probably just as a friend, of course—but that's more than I was expecting! He *likes me*!

I can feel myself blushing, alone on my spaceship in the middle of a galaxy. I feel like the stupidest teenage girl ever to exist, getting hysterical over a boy. A boy who likes talking to me so much that he can't help but tell me everything he feels.

It makes my stomach flip in a combination of excitement and nerves. It's a bit scary, in a grown-up, mature way. There's so much pressure, so much I don't know how to do. Things I've only ever read about in fics.

I can't think of anything that could make my life better right now. Except maybe for time to hurry up, for *The Eternity* to bring my J to me sooner.

We have everything in common. J is so thoughtful and

funny and cute. Talking to him is so easy. It's exactly how I imagined talking to a boy would be, back when I only had Jayden to practice on, in my imagination.

I want to make him happy more than anything else. As long as J is happy, everything will be OK.

From: The Infinity Sent: 10/23/2067
To: The Eternity Predicted date of receipt: 11/08/2067

J,

I feel the same way about writing to you. It's like everything I've been struggling to understand about myself just makes sense when I tell you about it. You make it hurt less. It's crazy how much I have to say to you every single day. I think we would definitely have been friends in another life. I don't know how we couldn't be.

Today I found a secret stash of chocolate in the stores. It was hidden behind some boxes of mushroom soup, near the ladder. I think it was my dad's secret supply. He had a massive sweet tooth, unlike my mother. He must have been hiding all the chocolate behind the soup he knew we wouldn't eat—I hate mushrooms—so that he could sneak off to eat it. I can just imagine him gorging on sweets before returning with salmon fillets for dinner, saying we needed to eat more healthily. The image makes me feel happy and sad and tired, all at once.

I hardly ever find chocolate in the stores, so I'd like to eat it, but I can't bear to. It would be like another part of him is gone forever. However much I've tried to keep him with me—not disturbing his bunk, his notebooks, his toothbrush and razor—every trace of him will disappear in the end, like he was never here at all.

We were all really happy when I was little. This ship wasn't some terrifying place to be, back then. I loved it. I would have been distraught at the thought of leaving.

My mother used to tell the kind of silly jokes that would make me and Dad laugh so hard we couldn't breathe. She taught me how to do origami, and after every meal I'd carefully collect up all the food packets and wash them, then unfold them to use as origami paper. We got obsessed with it—we made this whole zoo of animals.

They were both really great parents. Up until the astronauts died.

R xx

DAYS UNTIL *THE ETERNITY* ARRIVES:
120

I keep hearing the astronauts. They scratch at the hull of the ship with fingernails like claws, scurrying across the outside of the ship in a series of thudding bangs. At night they scrape at the airlock, filling my ears with the high-pitched squeal of metal when I'm trying to sleep.

I tell myself that it's just the noise of the engine, or space debris. But when I follow the sound, it stops. When I look out of the porthole, they hide. But I know they're there. They know I'm here, tracking them.

They freeze when I start listening. They don't want to be caught. The astronauts are clever. They're patient.

I'm getting desperate.

From: The Infinity   Sent: 10/28/2067
To: The Eternity   Predicted date of receipt: 11/12/2067

J,

There are so many changes happening on board *The Infinity*. I'm so ashamed that I can't cope with all the efficiency improvements, even though they're for the good of the ship.

The UPR have now asked me to only flush the toilet once a day, and reduce my showers to every two weeks. Even if they're short showers, I'm used to washing every other day. I'm going to smell awful if I only wash once a fortnight.

I suppose I'd better savor my last shower, because I'll have forgotten what it feels like by the next time I have one.

I can't wait until we can be together. You make me feel safe in a way that nothing else does anymore.

R xx

DAYS UNTIL *THE ETERNITY* ARRIVES:
106

By the time two weeks have passed and I'm allowed to take another shower, I'm desperate to wash. My hair feels like cardboard, and I've got acne all over my back and chest.

I tip my head back under the warm stream of water, memorizing the feel of it over my skin. It's pure heaven. I wash my hair four times to get rid of all the oil, rubbing my fingers over the strands and reveling in their new softness.

I can get used to infrequent showers, I suppose. It wasn't as bad as I'd expected. After the first week, I stopped noticing how I smelled. It was only really bad when I had my period. And it is for the good of the ship, after all.

But when I wash away the suds, I notice that my hands are covered in dark hair from my scalp. Layers of it twist around my fingers and follow the lines of my palms.

My hair is falling out. What if there's something wrong with me?

Soaking wet, I run to the computer and type "hair loss symptoms" into the medical subroutine. Holding my breath, I skim-read the list of causes:

MALE PATTERN BALDNESS
DRUG-INDUCED
STRESS

Hair loss is a symptom of stress. Understandable.

I hope it's limited to a few strands. I've never really cared what I look like—it's never really mattered before. But with J arriving, suddenly it does. I can't handle the thought of him seeing me and being . . . disappointed. What if J thinks my body doesn't live up to my personality? What if I'm so unattractive that he decides even our friendship can't make up for the way I look?

Taking careful breaths, I avoid thinking about it. If stress is causing the hair loss, then I'm only going to accelerate the process by worrying about it. I need to stay calm.

DAYS UNTIL *THE ETERNITY* ARRIVES:
104

Today is my birthday. I'm going to make a cake.

I scour the stores for chocolate pudding and brownies, which I mix into a sticky mess that I shape into something round and vaguely cake-like. I stir together sugar, water, and powdered milk to make a kind of icing, and scrape it on top of the chocolatey cake, curling it up into rough peaks. It's messy and inelegant, but it looks cheerful.

I don't have a candle to put on top—that's far too much of a fire hazard for space—but I twist up seventeen scraps of paper and stick them in the icing, coloring the ends a bright orange.

Seventeen. I feel a lot older.

As I pretend to blow out the candles, a wish flashes through my mind without me even needing to think about it: *I wish J were here.*

Then I stretch out in bed on my stomach and eat cake until I feel sick. I can't help wondering what my next birthday will be like. J will be here by then. I'll be turning eighteen.

Just the thought of J sends electric shivers from my fingers to the tip of my toes. I want him to kiss me. I want to feel his fingers wrapped in my hair.

I want *him*, not just his words; I want his body too. Writing letters isn't enough – it's never been enough.

I wonder whether J will give me a birthday present. A birthday kiss.

The thought deserves my complete attention. I roll over, and push my pajama bottoms off my hips.

DAYS UNTIL *THE ETERNITY* ARRIVES:
103

I think about sex a lot. Objectively, the idea is kind of disgusting—especially when you start learning about STDs and fissures and enemas. I get kissing—I understand that. I've kissed the back of my hand, and it seems kind of pleasant, so yeah. That makes sense. But . . . sex? I just can't figure it out.

I can't decide whether all the gross parts would fade away if you're with someone you really love, or whether you'd still notice things like *smells* and *noises* and *stickiness*, but the emotions overwhelm it all. I want to know a lot of things like that about sex, and I don't have anyone to ask.

I never thought it would matter to me anyway. It wasn't like I was ever going to have sex with anyone. But now . . . there's J.

J makes my heart feel like it's purring in my chest. I've been sending him the most honest, truthful secrets I have, and he still likes me. He might even like me enough to one day have sex with me.

In just over three months, we'll be meeting in person, face-to-face. I need to start getting ready so I look like the girls in films, all smooth and beautiful. I don't want to disgust him with my hairy eyebrows and legs and armpits. I want him to like me. I want him to see me as a woman.

I research how to pluck my eyebrows using beauty guru tutorials from decades ago. For the first time ever, I stand in front of the mirror, eyes watering, and pull hairs from my skin.

Copying a picture of Lyra Loch, I try to sculpt my brows into elegant arches, but all I manage to do is make myself look permanently surprised. I'm glad I started early, so I have time to practice.

Next, I shave my legs, and only nick myself three times. My legs feel smooth for a day, and then start to itch. It surprises me how quickly the hair grows back; sharp and blacker than before.

Even though he isn't here to see it, after my next shower I'm going to divide my wet hair into thin clumps and braid each one, so that it'll dry curly. I wish that I had makeup, so I could contour my cheekbones and extend my eyelashes with mascara.

I've used the fabric from the stores to make three skirts, two dresses, and one nightdress. My favorite is a dress I designed based on the one that Lyra wears in the episode where she and Jayden have to pretend to be married for a case.

It's beautiful. Every time I try it on, my stomach does flips. I keep picturing the way that Jayden looked at Lyra when she wore that dress. His jaw dropped, a pink flush tinging the tips of his ears as he ran a hand through his hair.

It's the way I've always wanted someone to look at me— with eyes full of awe and a smile that tries to hide it. When I imagine J seeing me wearing the dress, I can feel the fluttering pump of my heart against my ribs, lighter than air, and the rush I usually only get from reading cute fics fills my stomach.

I should make more clothes; a whole wardrobe of outfits for him to see me in. I have the time. When *The Eternity* arrives, I'll be ready.

DAYS UNTIL *THE ETERNITY* ARRIVES:

100

From: UPR   Sent: 02/15/2066

To: The Infinity   Received: 11/17/2067

Subject: For Attention of The Infinity

Attachment: Lighting-schedule.exe [30 KB]

Commander Silvers,

Following previous communications to undertake improvements to *The Infinity*, please reduce the vessel's temperature by one degree centigrade in all habitation areas, from 24°C to 23°C. This will save heating resources.

Please also limit light by 50 percent by installation of the attached lighting scheduling software to ensure optimum efficiency.

Thank you for your cooperation.

All hail the UPR! May the king live long and vigorously!

✳ ✳ ✳

I stare at my model farmhouse, which in the last few months has grown into a whole town made out of dinner packets. As well as my origami farm animals, I've populated it with people: a tiny Romy with a cutting of my hair glued onto a spoon head and ballpoint pen freckles, a J with cardboard limbs and a minuscule set of juggling balls, and a dozen children of different ages.

Model J is showing Model Romy how to plant seedlings outside the building. Nearby, a tissue-paper dog is digging up apple seed pebbles from the soil. A little boy is looking adoringly up at J, holding on to one trouser leg. There's a tiny cotton-wool baby in Model Romy's arms.

I've spent hours carefully building up my dream life. I've put all my hopes and desires and love into the model, wishing with every tinfoil or string addition that one day it will come true.

Right now it feels like it will never happen. I thought a year would fly by, every day bringing me closer to J. Instead, time has slowed down, turning to tar that keeps me trapped here away from him. It's an effort to get through a day.

I don't know how much longer I can keep waiting.

There's an ache, a throbbing in my skull, telling me that I'm cursed: by my mother, by the dead astronauts, by the UPR, by this ancient, failing ship.

They want me to turn off the lights for an extra four hours a day. The very idea makes me want to cry. I'll be cornered, alone and awake, waiting until my designated daylight hours begin. Anything could creep up on me and I'd have no idea.

I'm not going to do it. I'm going to ignore them. The UPR are light-years away—they can't force me to do it.

My brain doesn't seem to be listening. It skitters away from my insistence that I'm safe. Without any warning, I'm on the edge of a panic attack. I push my head into my sweaty palms, trying desperately to stop myself from doing this. My lungs seize up like there's a strap around my chest. I can hear myself making thick wheezing noises.

I won't do what they've asked. But even as I tell myself I won't, I know that I will. I'm the commander. I have to do anything it takes, even if it's a sacrifice, to look after my ship.

I'm going to have to turn off the lights.

My horror is so large it fills the room, pressing into every corner until there's no air left for me. There's no space to move. I can't breathe, can't make my limbs bend, can't even blink. I'm drowning.

I'm not strong enough to do this. Why couldn't someone else be here, in charge of this ship?

Anyone would be better than me.

That night I turn off the lights two hours earlier than usual and lie in my bunk, unable to sleep, straining my eyes to make out any traces of the ceiling in the black.

After an hour, the creeping panic gets too much for me and I fall into a fitful sleep.

DAYS UNTIL *THE ETERNITY* ARRIVES:
99

I wake up too early and can't make myself go back to sleep because I'm desperate for the toilet. I've been getting into the habit of turning on the lights while I run to the bathroom, then turning them off again until the extra hours of assigned power saving are up.

But when I try to turn on the lights this morning, they don't work. The UPR's new lighting schedule is automatic. It must not have an option that lets me override it.

I reach over to the side of my bed, fingers searching for the shaft of my flashlight. When I turn the light on, it glows a dull yellow for a few seconds and then switches off. Out of charge. There have been so many power cuts recently that I've been using it almost every day, and I must have forgotten to recharge it last night.

I'm stuck in bed until the lights come on, then. My tablet

is in the living area, so I can't even use that as a flashlight. The ambient light routine has been deactivated completely, so there isn't the usual dim pink light of simulated dawn. It's pitch-black, completely and utterly. I'll have to lie and wait.

My bladder complains insistently that it's achingly full. I cross my legs, shifting onto my back and trying to focus on anything other than my desperation to pee. I don't know how much longer it will be until the lights come on, until I can finally get out of bed. It might be an hour or more. I'm not sure I can make it.

I pin my fists to the bed and squeeze my eyes shut, pretending I'm still asleep, I'm still dreaming and I'm not ready to get up yet anyway.

My breath is shallow and quick. I'm asleep, *I am, I am, I am.*

I count to two hundred, then four hundred. I can't wait much longer.

I let out a frustrated sob. Every time I breathe in, I'm certain that I'm about to wet myself.

I have to go to the bathroom.

Carefully standing up, I curl my toes against the floor. I take a hesitant step with one hand reached out in front of me. I'm overcome with a desperate certainty that if I move now, I'll end up walking right into some rotting creature, or trip into a bottomless hole in the floor that wasn't there before.

I picture the layout of the furniture, hoping that I know my own bedroom well enough not to trip over anything. The five meters across the room feel like miles.

I catch my foot on the edge of a cabinet, and the impact ricochets up the bones of my calf. Ignoring the pain, I carry on walking, but my fingers touch a wall somewhere I didn't expect a wall to be. I think I lost my sense of direction when I crashed into the cabinet. I can't think, can't reorient myself.

In my blindness, I start imagining hands curling up over my shoulders; the moist breath of something standing just in front of me, motionless and waiting; the tickle of fingertips gliding only micrometers from my face.

Suddenly I can't breathe. I'm desperate for the lights to come on, to show me that the monster I've invented isn't real.

I stagger along the wall, hoping that somehow I'll find the entrance to the bathroom without falling into the pit of the living area, but I can't think about anything except slimy finger-nails and rotten breath.

My knees give out beneath me and I collapse against the wall, gasping and straining my eyes in the darkness. I hope desperately that the lights are seconds away from turning on, but nothing happens.

I curl up on the floor, my nightmares creeping toward me in this blackness. Frozen astronauts touch me, coming for me with eyes bulging from their sockets. Sobs rack my chest, tears spilling from my eyes. Before I can stop myself, or crawl any farther toward the bathroom, my bladder lets out.

When I feel warm liquid flood over my legs, I'm so ashamed

that my crying increases. Urine stings the insides of my thighs, smelling sharp in my nose. I can't handle even a few hours in the dark.

I try to ignore the pins and needles trailing across my skin. It feels like fingers are stroking me; like the astronauts have finally come for me. I don't have the strength to stop them. I close my eyes and let them take me.

The astronauts.

They had only been in stasis for seven years when the torpor technology started failing. The problem might have been something to do with the space radiation interacting with the oxygen-rich liquid that filled their lungs, or the artificial gravity microclimate, or something else completely. My parents never found out. It just happened.

Without any warning, without any way to stop it, the astronauts started dying in their sleep. One by one. Lights flicked off as lives passed silently into the night.

I was only four, but I can remember it. My parents tried desperately to hide their worry, but I knew something was wrong.

I remember Dad patting me absently on the head and telling me to stay in the living quarters when I asked if we could play hide-and-seek in the stores. It was obvious his mind was full of other things.

I followed him and watched from the doorway of the sick bay as they tried to wake up the astronauts, one after another. Most died before ever regaining consciousness. Later, I found out that the men and women who did survive the stasis were brain-dead. Humanity's cleverest minds had been wiped away.

There was nothing that could be done.

The only thing that survived was the embryos. The undeveloped cells were only ever supposed to be a way of ensuring genetic diversity on the new planet. Now they are Earth's only hope.

My parents didn't stop trying to save the astronauts, not until they'd woken up every single one of them and run MRI scans, searching in vain for brain activity.

I left when my mother started injecting the brain-dead. I crawled under my duvet and waited, eyes closed, listening as hundreds of souls left their bodies. It was the loudest silence I have ever heard.

My mother gave a euthanasia injection to every astronaut who survived torpor sleep. She killed almost the entire crew of The Infinity and she didn't cry, not once, the entire time. I couldn't understand why, back then. Now I know that there are just some things so terrible you can't cry about them, because if you start, you will never stop.

After the astronauts died, the three of us were alone. The ship was empty.

Before, it had been the best place in the entire world: filled with music and colored lights, and secret hiding places that were perfect for a little child to curl into, giggling as her parents searched for her.

After they died, it was dark and full of shadows, and so, so quiet.

When the astronauts left, so did the light from my mother's eyes. Dad told me that she just couldn't handle the trauma—not on top of the pressure, the isolation, and the confinement of being in space. My mother watched all their closest friends die one by one. She put them to sleep, unable to save them.

She developed an adjustment disorder—her mind rejected her reality.

I didn't understand that, not then. Not really now, either. How can a child understand that their mother has left them when she is right there in front of them? I used to cry and beg and plead for her to see me, to just *look* at me instead of at the astronauts she saw in her mind. But I could never bring her back to us. I wasn't good enough.

Dad tried to help, but there was nothing he could do. She was beyond help.

He tried.

There is a trail of bodies in the wake of *The Infinity*, and every one of them is watching me.

At night they enclose the ship, peering in through the portholes. Every dead astronaut—skin bleached white from radiation and leaking drops of greasy, iridescent cooling fluid from their nostrils—follows me when I sleep. They peer around corners, run their shriveled fingers down my spine. When they touch me, their desiccated flesh crumbles into dust, coating me in layers of sticky, ancient corpses.

The astronauts all hate me for doing what they couldn't and surviving. They whisper my name, shuddering, groaning, telling me that my parents' failure is my failure, that I'm cursed because they couldn't save them.

The dead crew of *The Infinity* gather together in clusters, forming a writhing ball of bodies, limbs entwined. They whisper threats in the vacuum of space. They grab on to the outside of the ship, trying to block the signal to the transmitter and cut off my messages from J.

The ghosts of *The Infinity* want me alone, so I have to pay attention to them. They want to crawl inside my head and inhabit my worst fears.

Dad's death was the first punishment. One day they are going to kill me too.

When the lights finally come on, I pull myself to my feet and stagger into the kitchen. I carefully don't think about how clammy and cold my pajamas feel, how my cheeks are sore with salt. I get changed, wishing desperately that this was a shower day.

I fall onto my bunk, staring up at the ceiling as I force down a cereal bar and try desperately not to close my eyes again.

***

J,

I've been dreaming more recently. I imagine the astronauts clinging to the outside of the ship. I know that logically there are no corpses in space—my dad put the bodies of the astronauts in body bags and froze them until the liquid evaporated. Then they were vibrated until they shattered into dust, in a kind of space cremation.

There are no corpses following me. If there's anything to be scared of, it's not their *bodies*. Those are just dust, hidden away in the stores.

But I keep dreaming about the astronauts, more and more. The same nightmares I've been having my whole life. I can't stop myself, however much I try.

I don't know why they scare me so much. I don't know why their memory just won't leave me in peace.

I hope I stop dreaming after you arrive. I hope that when I'm not alone anymore, my brain will be less determined to scare me in any way that it can.

R xx

DAYS UNTIL *THE ETERNITY* ARRIVES:
90

I'm finally getting used to the hours of darkness. I've got a bowl under my bunk for emergencies, and a charger for my flashlight, plus two spares. As long as I make sure not to open my eyes, then the lack of light doesn't trigger another panic attack. It isn't so bad.

I've also memorized all of J's emails, so during the black hours I can whisper them to myself, going over everything he's ever said to me, from the first "Dear Commander Silvers" to "Sometimes I feel like you're the only thing in my life that I can depend on."

I've saved so much energy from the extra four hours a day I've been sitting in the darkness. Energy that will go to the lights and computers.

I won't let this ship fall apart around me.

I can still hear the scratching outside the ship. There's something out there. It's trying to get in.

I follow the noise around the ship moving from room to room and listening as it scrambles across the outside hull. I'm certain that it peers into portholes when I'm not looking, trying to find a weak spot to get inside.

It's never going to stop trying. It works at the seals on the airlock, nails digging into the rubber to force it open.

I hope that J gets here before it manages to find a way in.

DAYS UNTIL *THE ETERNITY* ARRIVES:

82

From: The Eternity
To: The Infinity
Attachment: audio-subsystem.exe [13 MB]

Sent: 12/05/2067
Received: 12/05/2067

I have some exciting news for you, Romy! Now that there's only a few months until we can meet in person, *The Eternity* is currently slowing down to allow it to match *The Infinity*'s speed when the ships meet, so they will be able to connect.

That means the ships are finally close enough for us to audio chat! You just need to install the software I've attached, and it'll let us talk via audio. There will be a little time lag between replies, but it should be quite short—less than a minute, now that we're so close. It's worth giving it a try, anyway, right? Sadly we're not quite close enough for video chat yet, but we should be able to do that soon.

Is it OK if I call you tonight at 7 p.m.? If it isn't, just don't answer. But I hope you do. I've been waiting for this moment for so long. I haven't been able to think about anything but speaking to you. I can't wait to hear your voice.

J xx

My heart jumps into my throat and refuses to move. We can talk on the phone. *We can talk on the phone.*

J is calling me tonight!

I install the software he's sent me, which is a subsystem NASA mustn't have thought worth installing. There have never been any other ships to talk to before now.

I try to stay busy for the next five hours, but I keep finding myself daydreaming, gazing off into space and imagining what J might sound like. When I read his emails, I've always just heard Jayden's voice in my head.

I decide to take my shower a few days early. I know J won't be able to see me, but I want to *feel* clean. I want to feel ready. I need something to boost my confidence.

By seven o'clock, I'm so nervous and excited that my hands are trembling. I sit at the helm, staring expectantly at the screen.

As soon as the words INCOMING CALL appear, I panic. What do I say? Do I even remember how to speak? I can't remember the last time I spoke aloud.

I swallow back my fear and reach out to click ACCEPT.

The ringing stops, and there's a moment of silence.

"Hello?" a deep voice says, testing.

I close my eyes and picture Jayden: dark curls and sparkling eyes with lines around them from smiling.

"J," I say, ever so softly.

After a delay of twenty seconds—enough time for me to gather my thoughts but less time than I was expecting, considering the distance—I receive a reply. "Romy?"

I pull in a tight inhale. "I'm here."

My mind fuzzes while I wait for his response. I can't focus on anything but the timer on the screen, counting the seconds since our call started. It's hard to believe this is really happening.

"Romy. It's so damn good to hear your voice."

My breath catches in my throat. "Y-you too."

His voice is stronger than I expected. I was imagining soft, gentle, emotional—like his emails. But the voice in my head was Jayden's. It was never going to be accurate.

"I don't know what to say to you," I admit, after a pause when neither of us speaks, just breathe together. I can't tell if it's an awkward silence. Have we been messaging for so long that it's not possible for it to be uncomfortable? I don't know.

"Me neither," J replies. "I had all these things I was going to say, but my mind's gone blank."

I clear my throat. I feel hot. I made his mind go blank. Me. "How are you?"

"Well, Romy, right now I'm just desperate for the ships to join up. To see you in person."

"Me too." I say it quietly, almost scared to let him hear something that to me feels so big, so completely life changing.

But J just glides over it, like we're both on the same page, like it's obvious. "I think next week we'll be able to have video feeds too."

I close my eyes again, almost dizzy at the thought of seeing and hearing J at the same time. This is almost too much as it is.

"I wish time could go faster," I say.

"I know. Is it strange to know that I'm coming? I've never asked before. I can't tell how you feel. Maybe you hate the idea."

"Not at *all*."

He lets out a gust of breath. "Good."

"Do you know when you'll be arriving yet?" I want to work out the exact number of hours, minutes, and seconds until he's here. "Are you still on schedule to arrive on the twenty-fourth of February?" That's the date in the mission timeline that Molly sent me, nearly a year ago.

He grunts. "Yes." There's an awkward pause, then he says, "Listen, the computer is telling me that I have to go. I think we're still too far apart for long conversations."

"OK," I say, disappointed that this was over so fast, and relieved that I'll have time to process this new communication method before we talk anymore. "Can we— Are we allowed to talk again? Maybe tomorrow? At the same time?"

"Yes. Definitely. I'd love that. Good night, Romy."

"Good night, J."

After we end the chat, I stare up at the ceiling, beaming so widely that my face might crack in half. I spoke to J, and it was nothing like I'd imagined, and everything I've ever wanted. He's so perfect. He's so real. I can't wait to meet him.

DAYS UNTIL *THE ETERNITY* ARRIVES:
81

The next morning, all I can think about is talking to J again. We arranged to speak tonight, but that's hours away and I can't wait that long. I want to call him *now*.

I open up the audio communication program, hoping it won't take too long to learn how to initiate a transmission. On the main menu is the option to scan for transmitters within range of the ship. I start the search, chewing on my nails. By now, they're short stubs, torn away at the skin.

The Eternity pops up in the Contacts list, followed by a series of numbers—the International Celestial Reference Frame coordinates of the ship, probably, showing its position in space.

Available Contacts (1)

The Eternity [ICRFJ002133.9+472421] IM · Dial · Block

Reference coordinates aren't usually included in the communications software I use. I wonder how far away *The Eternity* is now—will the time lag be noticeably shorter today? On a map, how far apart would our ships look?

I wonder if there's a way to combine the communications software that J sent me with *The Infinity*'s guidance system. If I have the coordinates, there must be a way to display *The Eternity*'s location visibly. If I can set up a map, I could leave it running in the corner of the screen, and watch our ships get closer together until they finally meet and join as one. It would be so exciting to watch it.

I open up the guidance system, loading a map of the galaxy. Then I return to the communications software and export the code that controls the coordinate scanning. After some trial and error, I manage to import the code to the guidance system and create an almost functional mapping device.

I zoom in to the coordinates in the range [ICRFJ001500.0+300000] to [ICRFJ002400.0+500000], which I think should narrow the search field enough to pick up both my and J's ships visibly on the screen. Then I scan for nearby transmitters.

The Infinity pops up first, a tiny white oval on the black map. Then *The Eternity*'s icon appears, a blip that, to my disappointment, is still a huge distance away from *The Infinity*. I suppose closeness is relative in space. Just because we can talk now doesn't mean J's not still millions of kilometers away.

I'm about to shut down the map when another icon pops up on the screen. It's labeled *UPR*. It's in the same place as *The Eternity*.

I freeze, staring at the screen. The program must have made a mistake. The UPR's headquarters are on Earth—they definitely aren't in space with J and me.

It's such a strange, impossible error that I restart the scanner, unsure how it could have imagined that the UPR are close by. The second time, the results are the same. The UPR pops up alongside *The Eternity*.

I don't understand. I can't make sense of any of this. I stare at the screen as my brain refuses to accept what I'm seeing. It looks like . . .

I rub my eyes, then read it again.

There must be an error with the software. This can't be possible.

I shake my head and close down the program. It's kind of funny, in a way. *The Eternity* and the UPR are seventeen trillion kilometers apart. I force myself to smile. What a silly mistake.

Abruptly, I stand up and walk across the room. Then I stop and turn back to stare at the computer.

I should prove it's a mistake. Just to be absolutely certain. It will only take a few seconds. If I check the UPR's emails and find their real coordinates on Earth, then it will be obvious that the scanning software has it wrong.

After walking back to the computer, I go into my emails. I access the source code of the raw transmission data from the last email I received from the UPR, searching for the origin coordinates. They must be hidden somewhere in the code.

When I find them, the coordinates are listed as being somewhere in space again. Not on Earth at all. This isn't just a malfunction with the audio program or guidance software. This is . . . something else. Something I don't understand.

Going through the last ten messages from the UPR, I plot out the coordinates and display them on my map. Every message was sent from a different place. The coordinates follow a straight line between Earth and *The Infinity*, as if whatever is transmitting the messages is getting closer to me every time. The messages from the UPR follow the path of *The Eternity*.

The coordinates don't lie. Every message from the UPR is coming from the same route as *The Eternity*.

Nothing makes any sense. I check the origin coordinates of my messages from J, clinging desperately to the hope that there's been some kind of computer error.

Every email sent from J and the UPR has had matching coordinates for the last six months. Both have come from the same place every single time. How can the UPR be emailing me from *The Eternity*?

I can only think of one explanation, but my mind refuses to accept it. It's impossible.

Fear weighs down my ribs, forcing my breaths back inside my lungs instead of letting them free.

Someone on *The Eternity* has been sending emails to me as the UPR.

No.

It's insane. Even just the *idea* is a betrayal of J, of our friendship. I don't believe it. There's no way in the universe that J—my lovely, sweet, considerate J—would ever, *ever* do anything like this. He would never hurt me.

Would he?

I go back and check every single message the transmitter has picked up in the last year, lining them up on my map until the evidence is undeniable. They all come from *The Eternity*.

I stand up and start pacing the room again. How can I process what I've discovered in a way that makes sense?

Abruptly, I return to the computer. I add Molly's emails to the map, just to double-check that this isn't some weird problem with the transmission data. Her old messages are all sourced as coming from Earth, just as they should be. This isn't a strange quirk of the technology.

I keep adding messages, trying to find the moment the error began. Finally, I add the most recent messages from Molly, when she told me that a war was starting on Earth, so she wouldn't be able to talk to me for a while.

They came from *The Eternity*.

I redo my work to make sure I haven't made a mistake, but

it's correct. Molly's final messages came from *The Eternity*, not from Earth.

Those last few messages from her, telling me about NASA's communication problems and the war—they were emails, I realize in horror. Not her normal audio messages. I never heard her voice—her actual voice—say anything about the war. Only the emails did. The ones from *The Eternity*.

Was there ever even a war at all? Was the whole thing made up? Is the UPR even *real*? Or is it—

Is it fake?

I try to swallow. My mouth tastes of the iron-rich rush of blood. Maybe there's someone else on *The Eternity* sending these messages to me. It can't be him. It's not in J's nature to lie. Is it?

My brain can't keep up with all of the new discoveries. I'm shaking. I look over my shoulder, half expecting to see J there, staring at me.

I feel like someone's torn out my heart. There's a pounding, throbbing roar in my ears.

J did this. He invented everything. The political disputes. The communication problems. The war. The UPR.

Even as I think it, I don't believe it. There's no way that it was J. It's impossible.

But someone made it up. Someone has been lying to me. Someone on *The Eternity*. And—however much I wish it wasn't the case—that means it can only be him.

***

I curl up in my bunk, staring at the walls of my silent, helpless ship and trying not to sink into another panic attack.

This isn't right. Someone so lovely couldn't possibly have such horrible motives. Not my J: kind and tender.

Could they? Could he really be anything but my lovely J?

It's not true.

I can't let it be true.

My heart is fighting against my brain. I still don't believe that this is possible. I must have made a mistake.

I scour the data, reprocessing the raw binary code and checking it by hand to make sure there isn't a translation error.

I don't find anything.

If the UPR is made up, that means that all of their messages—their instructions about how to preserve power, fix the malfunctioning equipment, and make the ship more efficient—are actually from J.

Why would he do that? Why would he bother to invent a war and a new government like the UPR and then just use them to help me make *The Infinity* better? He could have told me what to do himself, without using the UPR at all. It doesn't make any sense. Unless . . .

Oh no. No, no, no, no, no, no.

The program. The new operating system—the one the UPR sent me. The power cuts only started after the new software was installed. The UPR were the ones who told me there was even a problem with my ship at all.

If it was actually from J . . . what did he do to it?

Why would he want to update my software? Did he add any subroutines to the new version?

Were there *ever* any real problems? Or did J manipulate that? All those times when the ship failed, when the lights and heating system turned off. Was that on purpose, to torment me?

It's possible there was never an energy problem. It could all have been faked. If so, he stopped me from showering, from using the lights. I can't even imagine what kind of person would ever want to do that to another human being. It's torture. Physical and psychological torture.

Unable to breathe properly around my fear, I search for a way to remove the software from the computer, to return it to the old version. But it's gone. It was deleted months ago to make room for the new OS.

I'm stuck with J's program running my ship. Does he have access to it? He might be able to see everything I'm doing. Is he watching me, right at this moment?

I go into the software's settings and try to deactivate it. I've wasted so much time following his stupid, pointless rules. I can't let him control me. Not anymore.

The most I can do is limit the OS's permissions to make sure it doesn't do anything dangerous, like shut down the life-support systems. I can't stop it from causing power cuts. Every single time the lights flicker out, it will remind me of how stupid I was to fall for his lies. Romy the Gullible.

∗ ∗ ∗

At lunchtime, I hear the *ding* of the arrival of two new emails. It takes me over an hour to summon the courage to read them. I brace myself, trying to convince my brain that I don't feel scared anymore, that this isn't affecting me. It's only words, after all. I should be able to handle that. If I were strong enough, this would all slide off me.

The worst thing is that I know if J says something gentle and sweet and tender, I won't be able to stop my heart jumping, even when I know the evil behind it. I still want him. I hate myself for it.

I swallow back a reflux of acid and open the first message.

From: UPR   Sent: 03/05/2066
To: The Infinity   Received: 12/06/2067
Subject: For Attention of The Infinity

Commander Silvers,

In order to adhere to efficiency rulings, we request that the ambient temperature of *The Infinity* should be lowered an additional two degrees centigrade, from 23°C to 21°C, to conserve energy.

This may cause some discomfort while your body acclimatizes, but please wear more clothing in the meantime.

All hail the UPR! May the king live long and vigorously!

From: The Eternity   Sent: 12/06/2067
To: The Infinity   Received: 12/06/2067

Romy,

It was so nice talking to you yesterday. I'm looking forward to speaking to you again tonight.

I want to hear more about the UPR. It's really worrying me that you're suffering when I can't do anything to help. I hate the thought of them upsetting you. You're stronger than you realize. I believe in you, Romy Silvers.

J xxx

It's sickening. My chest aches; a dull throb like I've bruised it. Only a matter of hours ago, I was desperately in love with J, and now I can't see anything but how horribly fake his messages are.

He's sending me these unnecessary requests from the UPR and then pretending that he's worried about me doing them, all at the same time. He's using the UPR to twist me up, to torment me.

J has been lying to me the whole time that I've known him. He's had me wrapped around his little finger for months. It's obvious now.

I can't ignore the evidence, or what it means. He faked the UPR. He invented the war. He's made me spend almost a year worrying and panicking and obsessing over what was happening to the people on Earth.

He couldn't have done that for any reason other than cruelty. He's been tormenting me long distance, the only way that he can. Everything the UPR made me do—from sitting in darkness until I wet myself to living covered in grease and sweat without showering—was really because of J. He made up a complicated lie and even took over my computer so he could do those things to me.

How could he put me through that? Why would he even want to?

I read every email, desperate for some evidence that our connection is real, that it can't be J doing this. A particular line from one of his recent messages jumps out at me:

I wonder if we would have been friends if we had been meeting in less exceptional circumstances. I hope so. I really do, neighbor.

Something about that particular phrase sounds familiar. *Meeting in less exceptional circumstances.*

I can't place it. I think about it all afternoon. Where have I heard that before?

Then it hits me: it's a line from one of my fics.

Jayden says that to Lyra, in a fic I wrote back before I ever met J.

"You're OK," he said, his voice a low, calming murmur in her ear. "Relax."

Lyra sagged under his—very solid—chest.

"Thanks," she said, her voice cracking in an embarrassing way. "I'm Lyra."

"Jayden. It's great to meet you, neighbor," Jayden continued. "I just wish we were meeting in less exceptional circumstances!"

* * *

I wrote that line. And J used it in an email to me.

It might just be chance, but . . . it's exactly the same.

I check the date I sent the fic to Molly and run some calculations. The transmission would have crossed *The Eternity*'s path almost six months ago—giving J more than enough time to pick up the transmission, read it, and include a quote in an email to me.

Is that possible? Would he really do that? Even now, I'm hoping that it's a coincidence.

I read J's emails again one by one, carefully analyzing the words.

I find ten more lines, taken word for word from Jayden's dialogue in my other fics.

Is it OK if I call you tonight at 7 p.m.? If it isn't, just don't answer. But I hope you do. **I've been waiting for this moment for so long. I haven't been able to think about anything but speaking to you.** I can't wait to hear your voice.

"I've been waiting for this moment for so long," Jayden said, nose pressed into her cheekbone. "I haven't been able to think about anything but speaking to you."

I want to hear more about the UPR. It's really worrying me that you're suffering when I can't do anything to help. I hate the thought of them upsetting you. **You're stronger than you realize. I believe in you, Romy Silvers.**

"You're stronger than you realize. I believe in you, Lyra Loch."

Don't you give up on me, Romy, not yet. I'm coming—**just hold on a little longer.** It will be easier when we're together.

"Lyra! Don't you give up on me, Lyra, not yet. I need you. Just hold on a little longer."

I keep finding more. I can't find an email where J *hasn't* copied something from one of my fics. Not one. Even his earliest messages contain lines from fics I wrote when I was thirteen, sent to Molly long before I even knew *The Eternity* existed.

He's been using my own words against me.

The bile rises in my throat and I run to the bathroom and vomit until my stomach is empty. Then I press my sweaty forehead against the side of the toilet seat and cry until I feel like there's nothing left inside me but fear.

Why? Why would he—

Was he pretending to be Jayden? Was he trying to make me like him by mimicking Jayden Ness?

If he has been pretending to be Jayden this whole time, then who am I even talking to? A scream bubbles up in my throat and gets trapped somewhere behind my tonsils, sharp and terrified.

If everything I thought I knew about J is fiction (made up by *me*), then who is J at all? *Who is he?*

Who is this person who forges messages from Earth and creates something as horrible as the war and the UPR? Why would anyone ever *pretend to be a fictional character*?

Why would he spend all this time playing with me? Who am I talking to?

He took a character that he knew I liked and adored. He posed as him. He made me like him, made me *love* him.

He's been trying to destroy me, piece by careful piece, while I romanticized every second of it.

For the first time, the number of days until *The Eternity* catches up with me aren't exciting—they're terrifying.

Eighty-one days.

That's it.

I try to increase the speed of the ship, rerouting power to the thrusters to stretch out the time left before we meet, but *The Infinity* is already traveling at its maximum speed. There's nothing I can do.

In only a few months I'm going to have to meet whoever is on board the other ship. I'm going to have to face him, after everything he's done to me.

I can't trust anything he says, not anymore. I don't even know who I'm talking to. If he's lied to me about this, then what else?

I have no idea what to do, no way of even beginning to make a plan. How can I stop him coming for me? How can I escape?

I can't.

***

At seven, a shrill ringing sound comes from the computer. J's calling. Right on schedule.

I'm not going to answer it.

There's no way I can talk to him. I can't hear his voice and pretend I don't know what he's doing to me. I'll sound like a completely different person than I did yesterday.

I shudder and squeeze my eyes shut, like that will get me out of this, like if I just try hard enough I can erase time and make it so that *The Eternity* was never launched at all.

I crawl into my bunk and pull the duvet over my head until I'm safe in my cocoon of bedding, where I can ignore the computer and nothing can hurt me.

It rings and rings and rings.

I curl a pillow around my head to try and block out the shrill wail. It vibrates through me. It seems to last forever.

Finally, *finally*, it stops.

I lie back, stare at the ceiling, and try to catch my breath. Before I've even relaxed, the ringing starts again, loud and piercing and insistent.

I start to cry. He's not going to stop. Not until I answer. He's never going to leave me alone.

He calls three more times.

There must be a way to turn it off. When the ringing stops, I go to the helm. I try to block the calls, but as I'm clicking he rings again and—

My click accidentally answers the call—or perhaps I just

needed to *know*, once and for all, whether he's good or bad or somewhere in-between—and the ringing stops.

"Romy?" a voice says. The sound drags right up against my nerve endings.

My heart stops in my chest. I hold my breath, as if that will make him go away, as if he'll think it's an error and the call never connected at all.

"Are you there?" he whispers in a low croon.

I choke on a gasp.

There's barely a second of silence. The time lag has disappeared almost completely.

"You *are* there," he says. "I can hear you."

I swallow back stomach butterflies and moths and snakes, and before I can decide to end the call without saying a word, he says, "It's just me. There's no need to be afraid."

His voice is deep and terrifyingly gentle, as if he thinks by keeping it mild he can coax me into his arms. The sickening thing is that a day ago, it would have worked.

"I'm not afraid," I blurt out, without thinking.

There's another moment of silence. This time it seems victorious.

"I didn't think you were going to answer," he says eventually, slightly disapproving and slightly pleased.

It's only because I'm still not entirely convinced that he's done what I think he's done that I reply. "I wasn't. I answered by accident."

"You *are* scared." His words are absolutely certain. It sends a shiver down my spine so hard that it seizes up my neck.

"I have to go," I say quickly.

"See you so—" he says, but I end the call before he can finish talking.

I stare at the screen, panting and sweating like I've run four laps of the ship. I'm certain now. J isn't good. I never want to hear that voice again.

He calls again, but only once.

I sit cross-legged on the floor and stare at my model buildings, populated by the tiny Romy and the tiny J and the tiny little children we were going to raise together—in some alternative universe, where he was good and I was normal, and we were in love for real instead of for play.

I pick up the dinner-packet model farmhouses, which tilt on their glue foundations. Tiny paper chickens fly off the sides.

I carry the fragile creation to the airlock and leave it in the outer chamber. When I open the door, the model tears itself apart, twisting and turning until my future disappears into nothing.

DAYS UNTIL *THE ETERNITY* CATCHES UP:
80

I spend the day pacing the ship, buried waist-deep in hopeless solutions.

Eighty days. I still have eighty days. He's not here yet. I say it to myself over and over, trying to calm down.

Whichever way I look at it, I can't escape. How do you get away from someone flying toward you at nearly the speed of light? How do you avoid someone who can outrun you? How do you outmaneuver someone who has had over two years to plan?

Today, while I was searching through J's operating system, I found an audio file hidden in the coding. The room filled with the sound of fingernails scratching across metal when it played—just like the noises I've been hearing outside the ship.

The noises weren't in my head. I haven't been imagining things. He set up a program that played the sound at night.

The monsters were real. The monsters were created by J all along.

He must have spent hours on that one small thing to hurt me. And that's only the beginning. J's spent so much time and energy trying to make my life miserable. From the UPR to the power cuts, he's created the worst living conditions possible.

Is it even worth attempting to stop him? I wonder, still pacing the ship's corridors. He's coming, and there's nothing I can do about it. I could just wait and hope that when he arrives things will be different. But is that possible?

There's an abrupt silence as the sound of my echoing footsteps disappears. I realize I've stopped outside the sick bay without meaning to. I'm so tense that it almost makes me jump.

I stare at the half-open door.

There are so many places on the ship that I avoid because I'm afraid of facing the past. But the past is much less scary than the future. I know what's already happened; I know how bad it was. I don't know what's coming, though.

I breathe in the stale air and consider whether to step inside.

I was eleven when I heard a noise in the gene bank. I needed some help from Dad with an astrophysics problem, so I'd gone looking for him. When I went inside to see if it was him, I discovered my mother instead.

She was destroying the embryos, hitting the cases with the

oxygen tank from her suit. She smashed the glass, sending the contents pouring out across the floor in an icy mist of liquid nitrogen.

She turned to look at me, blood running down her wrist, fragments of glass sticking out of her fist. Stepping toward me, she ground the shattered remains of test tubes under her bare feet.

There was a blank look in her eyes, the way she always looked during a psychotic episode. "It's no good. It's not safe. We *can't do it*."

"Mum? What are you—" I didn't take my eyes off her, but yelled "DAD!" as loudly as I could.

My mother had been suffering from an increasingly violent psychosis for years, but I'd never seen her like this before.

"They don't get to choose!" she shouted.

"Who are 'they'?" I asked. I heard the sound of footsteps. Dad was coming.

"They shouldn't live on that broken, lonely world," she said, turning to stroke the door of the freezer, eyes on the samples inside.

"Talia!" Dad yelled as he reached the gene bank. "What are you—" He caught sight of the broken case behind her. "Oh God, no, Talia, what have you done?"

My mother jerked her head up. *"It wasn't their decision to make!"*

She raised the oxygen cylinder to the glass of the next

freezer, containing hundreds more embryos.

The tank hit the metal side and fractured on impact, oxygen escaping free of the canister in a loud hiss as shards of metal flew across the room.

She just raised her arms and aimed for the glass once more.

"TALIA!" Dad leapt at her, wrapping his arms around her shoulders, grabbing her fists before she could strike.

She let out a furious, mournful wail and threw all her weight forward. "It's too cruel. *We can't!*"

They wrestled, pulling each other in opposite directions, until Dad skidded on the mess on the floor. He crashed down, my mother falling on top of him.

She jerked away, pulling free of his grasp and diving for the nearest case. He grabbed at her arm, both of them slippery with blood. She turned on him, wild with fury, and pushed him away.

Dad's head jerked back as he fell, cracking against the sharp edge of one of the smashed freezer doors.

My mother hissed at him, "We deserve to die for what we did."

Dad made a broken, gasping noise that sounded like "Romy" and "help." I realized that he wasn't moving; that his head was bent at an unnatural angle. Blood dripped down the curve of his neck, fresh and black and thick. I ran to him, pushing past my mother.

"Stop it! Mum, he's hit his head!"

She just stared at me, like she couldn't understand who I was.

A shard of glass had pierced Dad's neck, gouging deep under the skin at the base of his skull. When I met his gaze, his pupils were blown wide; almost completely black.

"He's stuck, help me!" I yelled at my mother, the doctor, but I couldn't get her to move.

"They don't deserve this hell!" She forced the words out through her tears. "We should have ended this nightmare years ago!"

I fluttered my hands over Dad's head, trying to decide whether to pull him free of the glass. I had no idea how deeply it was lodged inside his head, but the blood flow was speeding up.

All I knew about first aid was that I had to stop the bleeding; I had to bandage him up. I was only eleven.

I carefully pulled his head away from the freezer door, trying to slide the glass out of his skin. It slid free a few centimeters, but then there was an unmistakable snapping sound. Dad turned frighteningly, sickeningly white. His pupils went blank. His chest fell flat.

My mother seemed to come back to herself then. She stopped screaming and stared down at Dad like she couldn't understand what had happened.

I knew before she did. He was dead.

My mother turned to look at me with empty eyes. I felt

certain that she was coming for me next.

I ran.

In the corridor, I climbed the ladder up to the stores, expecting her to grab hold of my legs at any moment. I climbed until I reached a gap between two shelves and dived inside, crawling as deep as I could get, squeezing myself into a space too small for anyone but an eleven-year-old.

I could hear noises behind me, banging and crashing. I didn't know if she was chasing me or still smashing up the embryo freezers, but I didn't turn to check.

Lying in the darkness, I could feel blood ooze from my kneecaps where I'd grazed them on food packets. Every time I breathed, my chest touched boxes on either side of me.

I listened.

I stayed there for two days; listening, waiting, certain that my mother was coming for me.

I hid in the utter blackness of the stores until I was too thirsty to wait any longer, until the memory of Dad's eyes turning blank as I held him was too much to bear, alone in the dark.

When I climbed back down to ground level, the ship was completely silent. I stood in the corridor, trying to decide what to do. My mouth was parched, but my brain was telling me to find out where my mother was before I went to get a drink.

I couldn't hear anything. After ten minutes, I slowly walked down the corridor to the habitation area, the sound of my own footsteps making me jump.

It was empty.

I checked in the cupboards, under the bunks. When I was sure I was alone, I went to the sink and drank and drank and drank. Then my fear came back in a rush.

I thought about just going back up to the stores with a bottle of water, but the ship was so silent and empty that my curiosity got the better of me. I needed to know what my mother was doing—and part of me wanted to find Dad. Because I hadn't entirely convinced myself that he was actually dead.

I checked the entire ship. The only sounds were ones that I made.

The gene bank was empty—and it had been cleaned. There was no trace of the accident, except for the smashed cases. The others were intact, full of hundreds more embryos that hadn't been destroyed.

If I'd looked harder, I might have found the fragment of my mother's oxygen tank, engraved with her name, hidden in the doorframe. I was too confused to do anything but carry on wandering the ship.

I didn't know what to think.

The last place I checked was the sick bay—some tiny, hopeful part of my brain thinking that Dad might be recovering there, with my mother tending to him.

When the door slid open, my eyes immediately found the jar of ashes waiting on the table.

Dad.

I took a tentative step into the room, forcing my eyes away from the jar, searching for my mother. I knew she must be in here. I'd looked everywhere else.

The room was empty.

"Mum?" I called, my voice breaking, barely louder than a whisper.

No reply.

I swallowed. The room was lined with the empty stasis pods: silent upright memorials to the astronauts who had died in them. There were nearly a hundred. Was my mother hiding in one of them—or waiting to creep up on me while I checked them?

I had to look. I had to find her.

I started opening the pods one by one.

Empty.

Empty.

Empty.

The tenth pod I checked wasn't empty. Even worse, it was running. According to the monitor displaying vital signs, there was someone inside.

I was flooded with adrenaline. I braced myself and opened the door. My mother was inside. She was in stasis, like the astronauts had been before the failure.

I stared at her for long seconds. I couldn't look away from her eyelids, frozen shut. I expected her to open them at any moment and lunge for me.

When the machine started beeping at me to shut the door before defrosting occurred, I closed it and backed away, dropping to the ground and staring at the pod.

My mother had tidied up the gene bank, cremated Dad, and then checked herself into a pod and entered torpor sleep.

She knew the risks, but she had done it anyway.

I still don't know why. Guilt? Terror? Panic? Or just madness?

I don't know. I hope I never find out.

I stored Dad's remains alongside the astronauts' ashes. Touching the fine grains of his ashes was when I first realized that I was alone. Forever.

I haven't been back to the sick bay since then. I don't want to know if she's still alive. I don't want to know whether I'm sharing my ship with a murderer or a corpse.

I don't want to know why she put herself into stasis.

I never want to see her again.

I stare at the neat lines of pods through the open door of the sick bay. I understand now why my mother wanted to destroy the embryos.

She thought that it was better to never live at all than to live in the world as she saw it—where you were forced to watch your friends die, and had to cling to tiny fragments of human communication from a planet an ever-increasing number of light-years away.

She thought it was kinder to destroy the cells before they

had a chance to suffer through what we had experienced—or worse. Is no life at all better than the constant fear and fight for survival I face every day?

I don't know.

If a life of fear isn't worth living, then why should I carry on? It's not possible to be more afraid than I am right now. The thought of J coming for me hurts to the marrow of my bones in a deep primal dread.

Whatever happens, I can't see a point in time when I will ever be happy. For the rest of my life, I'll be struggling. I'm always going to be moments away from sinking completely.

So why should I live at all?

I could do what my mother did, and just . . . not. Check into a pod. Leave my life up to chance. Refuse to take responsibility.

It would be so easy. But it would be so *pointless*. Every year I've fought to survive would be wasted.

I realize then that I've made up my mind: I want to live. I want to live so much that I would tear out the throat of anyone who tried to stop me. I'm not going to give up. I'm not going to sit back and wait for J to find me and play more of his games.

I'm going to fight. I'm going to do whatever it takes to survive.

DAYS UNTIL *THE ETERNITY* CATCHES UP:
79

I'm hiding in the stores again. Pressed up against the ceiling, I strain my eyes for any sign of the shadow of my mother coming for me.

I hear her quietly calling my name, and at first I think she's far away in the distance. Then I feel a hand on my ankle and realize it was a whisper.

She tugs, fingernails digging into my skin.

"Come on, Romy. Come out and play."

It's not my mother at all. It's J. He leans over me, his breath foul and rotten. He stares at me with Jayden's face and J's voice, laughing maniacally in short bursts.

"Hello there, Romy," he says, and—

I wake up.

I lean over the side of my bunk and vomit, coughing up the

last few lumps of food and stomach acid, then spitting onto the floor.

My heart is racing. My head hurts so badly that it's like I've been stabbed in the skull.

It's only when I'm calm that I realize I woke up because I heard a noise: an enormous, echoing bang.

I strain my eyes against the darkness, trying to work out if the sound is real or if it's another of J's software tricks. Everything is silent and still, except for the dull thud of blood against my eardrums. I stare at the ceiling for long, agonizing minutes, certain that his scratching creatures are back again, crawling across the outside of the ship. I've turned off the audio feed, but maybe it's another subroutine.

Then there's a slow, steady creak.

I bolt upright.

Emergency lights flicker on around me as I run to the helm. It's glowing bright red with a warning message.

VESSEL ATTEMPTING TO CONNECT

DETERMINE STATUS

A vessel. Connecting? I don't understand.

The computer flashes up a new message:

VESSEL IDENTIFICATION DETERMINED

ALLOW "THE ETERNITY" TO CONNECT

The Eternity.

The noise. That was *The Eternity*, touching my ship. It's months too early. But somehow . . .

It's here.

My brain engages all at once.

"No!" I yell at the computer, frantically typing commands. "DO NOT ENGAGE. DO NOT ALLOW ACCESS."

CONNECTION WITH "THE ETERNITY" INITIATED

"No! No! No! DO NOT CONNECT."

I push buttons, canceling and denying every message that comes up, but the software is J's software, so of course it doesn't listen to me. I should have tried harder to get rid of it.

J lied to me. When he said on our call that he wouldn't be arriving for a couple of months, he was only a few hours away. He knew. He knew he would be seeing me tonight.

He was playing with me.

Yet another game.

The computer keeps refusing my commands. *The Eternity* overrides every instruction I give it, initiating safety checks and air equalization procedures until:

VESSEL CONNECTED SUCCESSFULLY
AIRLOCK SEAL DECOMPRESSING

A hot flush shoots across my shoulder blades.

"DO NOT OPEN THE AIRLOCK. NO. NO!"

There's nothing I can do to stop it. The computer won't let me.

I run to the airlock. If I'm fast enough, I might be able to disengage it manually. I skid to a halt in front of the lock, just in time to see the outer door slide open.

A figure is standing in the doorway.

J and I stare at each other through the glass of the inner door. Behind him I can see the inside of the other ship, glowing with white light, all steel and curving lines.

He steps forward into the repressurized airlock. The inner door detects his movement and slides smoothly open. J steps on board *The Infinity*.

It isn't the way he looks that surprises me—even though he is nothing like he described, looks nothing like Jayden at all, which I should have realized was just another thing he told me to try and trick me. It's his eyes. His eyes are victorious. He thinks he's already won.

He's so *big*. So much bigger than I was expecting. Blond, muscular, stubbled. I tug my nightdress down over my thighs.

We stare at each other. For too long, neither of us speaks. We watch. We wait.

Then I turn and run.

I don't look back, not even to check if he's following me. I'm fast, I know I'm fast. With a head start, I can outrun him. I know the ship, and he doesn't. I can lose him.

I just keep running, running, running. Around the corridor to the other side of the ship, up the ladder to the stores, through the tunnel between the stacks. Some instinct tells me that because I was safe here last time, I'll be safe here again.

I can't think. I can't even catch my breath for fear.

I crawl as fast as I can, deep into the bowels of the ship. I can't hear him behind me, so I must be safe. I must be alone.

I take a left and a right and another left, weaving between the stacks of supplies into the labyrinth. I clamber up on top of a low pile of packets of lasagna and hit a wall. I've reached the center of the ship. There's nowhere else for me to go.

I crawl along over the top of the stack and drop down into a crevice between the boxes and the side of the ship.

I listen. There's only silence. I quickly block up the entrance with some containers. Unless you're looking carefully, you can't even see there's a gap here at all. There's no way he'll find my hiding place, at least not straightaway. I'm safe.

I crawl away from the entrance until it disappears out of sight around the curve of the ship's wall, so that if he does find it, he won't even see me.

Then I lean back against the steel wall, silent tears dripping from my jaw, barely able to stop myself from crying out loud.

I'm still shocked by how J looks.

He's short.

He's older than I'd pictured—definitely not twenty-two, like he claimed. He must be over thirty.

And he's gorgeous.

He has blond hair curling over his forehead and carefully cultivated stubble, and bulging muscles, and bright blue irises.

But his eyes. His eyes were trained on me like he was a predator and I was his prey.

Why would he describe himself as something he wasn't?

Surely you only lie if you're ugly, or old, or fat. But he's—

He's none of those things.

So why did he lie? It must be because he gets a thrill from it. I thought it was because he was trying to make me love him, but that wasn't the point at all. The lying was the point.

He was just playing with me. Every single thing about J was fabricated.

I curl my arms around my head, resting my forehead against my knees. I want to block out my thoughts, because everything going through my head is just making me panic more; and once I start I won't be able to stop, and then I'll be hidden in the dark in the stores in my nightdress, unable to breathe.

Why didn't he chase me? Why did he just stand there and let me go? After all the effort he took to sneak up to my ship while I was sleeping and catch me unawares. Why did he let me get away like that?

Because he doesn't need to chase me. There's nowhere I can run to escape him. We're on a ship in the middle of space. He's got me trapped.

I wonder what he's doing, whether he's even looking for me. An image of him searching through my things slithers into my brain. He could be poking his fingers in my hairbrush, touching my handmade clothes, stroking my teddy bear, toying with my models, eating my strawberry jam. . . .

I can't help but let out a horrified sob.

Why is he doing this to me? *Why me?*

How did he even get sent on this mission? Surely NASA must have put him through some kind of . . . *sanity test*? How did someone like him manage to be chosen for the second ever deep-space mission?

My mind goes around in circles, thinking over everything until I can't think anymore. Eventually, I close my eyes.

HOURS SINCE *THE ETERNITY* CAUGHT UP:

1

I'm halfway toward a kind of exhausted sleep when I hear a crackle. Every muscle in my body tenses, wondering what is coming next.

A voice echoes across the cavernous stores.

"Hello, Romy."

I bring my hands to my mouth to hold in a gasp. It's impossibly loud. It's like his voice is all around me. Where is he?

"I found the intercom."

I didn't even know there *was* an intercom. I press my head against the wall, half in relief that he isn't here in person, half in increased fear. He can talk to me whenever he wants. He can torment me for twenty-four hours a day.

"I'm sorry I scared you. I thought"—he lets out a laugh, short and obviously fake, crackling over the speakers—"that it would be a nice surprise for you, for me to arrive early."

I want to push my fingers into my ears, to block out the sound of his voice, but I can't. I need to know what he says.

"I can understand why you ran. But it's OK, you can come out now. I'm not going to hurt you. You know me. I only want what's best for you. I just want to say hello, after all this talking by email!"

He pauses, for long enough that I think it's over. When he speaks again, it makes me jump. His voice is low, almost inaudible.

"There's no need to rush, though. Take your time. I'm going to sleep now."

Then there's a crackle as the intercom shuts off.

Is he *in my bed*? The thought makes me feel like I'm covered in bugs, a literal itch on my skin.

Does he still think I don't know? How can he possibly think I haven't guessed, after I cut short his call? After I ran away from him?

How can he believe there's anything he can say that'll make me come out?

What am I going to do?

What am I going to do?

I can only stay here until my thirst makes me leave the stores in search of water. I have a day, maybe less. Long enough to come up with a plan. Probably.

Right now I don't believe there's any way I can win.

I curl up on the floor, rest my head on a lasagna tray, and

close my eyes. I take deep breaths in and out, pretending to myself that I'm asleep and not actually straining my ears for the slightest sound, or braced for action, on the edge of a panic attack.

After an hour, my muscles ache from the tension.

HOURS SINCE *THE ETERNITY* CAUGHT UP:
5

He gives me four hours, and then the intercom begins again. His voice is light and soft, almost a whisper.

"Good morning, Romy. Did you sleep well?" There's a pause, as if he's expecting me to answer.

I shiver, but not from the cold.

"Please come out?" His voice suddenly turns into a gentle croon. "I miss you. I miss our conversations."

Another pause. Then, "*Please. I've waited so long to meet you.*"

I bury my face in my hands, wishing I was less scared so that I could cry.

HOURS SINCE *THE ETERNITY* CAUGHT UP:
9

He doesn't stop pleading with me all morning. His voice has taken over my brain. It's worse than any nightmare.

"You're killing me here. If you don't come out, I don't know what I'll do. I might hurt myself. I'm in so much pain. . . ."

His voice grates at me, tearing away shreds of my control until I'm a fearful wreck. He's got me surrounded, wrapped up in his words. He's squeezing me tighter until I want to explode just to get free of the pressure. I can't escape.

I can't even stop listening.

HOURS SINCE *THE ETERNITY* CAUGHT UP:
13

"Please just talk to me, Romy. Say something. I need to hear your voice. I'm worried you've hurt yourself."

I wonder what he's doing—whether he's looking for me, wandering around my ship while he talks into the intercom. He could be doing anything, and there's no way I could stop him.

HOURS SINCE *THE ETERNITY* CAUGHT UP:
17

"Romy, you're being very silly. It's rude to ignore me like this."

I lie on my back and stare up at the crack between the wall and the edge of the stacks, where a grayish tinge of light encroaches on the blackness. My mouth tastes of bile and iron and mucus and salt.

HOURS SINCE *THE ETERNITY* CAUGHT UP:
19

"Don't you trust me? Do you think I'm going to hurt you?"

I'm going to die. This is it. I have to accept it. I have no plan; no way of escaping him. Nothing to do except go to him.

"Come out, Romy."

Why shouldn't I? I'm just delaying the inevitable, hiding here like a coward instead of facing my worst fear.

Right?

HOURS SINCE *THE ETERNITY* CAUGHT UP:
23

His voice is rough now, after hours of murmuring and begging. All of the kindness and gentleness is gone.

"I'm going to give you one last chance to come out, Romy. And then I'm coming to find you."

I press my palms into my eyes and bite down on a scream. I can't face him. He's going to kill me. And he knows I know—he's not even pretending anymore. He's coming.

I can't blink for fear.

He won't find me, whatever he says. He can't, not here. It's impossible.

I'm safe, I know I am.

My face is wet with tears.

He can't—

There's a noise.

The stacks all shift like they're falling, and I think for a moment I must have knocked into one and set off an avalanche, but then I see the light. It flickers across my hiding place, sending shadows dancing.

It gets brighter and brighter until a hand bursts through the boxes, then an arm and a head.

The head turns slowly, so slowly.

J looks at me. He smiles.

I catch sight of his wide grin before he shines his flashlight directly at me. It's so bright that I'm blinded. That kick-starts me. I throw myself backward along the side of the ship, straining to see past the bright spots in my vision.

A shadow lunges at me. Fingers grasp at my kneecap, skittering over bare skin and clasping around my calf.

His grip is tight when he tugs, pulling me closer. I let out a horrified scream and try to grab on to boxes, but he's too strong. I slide toward him, packets falling around me.

I can feel his breath, hot against the inside of my knee.

I kick out with my foot and connect with something solid. He grunts, his grip loosening. I do it again before he can stop me. I can feel something wet on my toes.

I dive backward, twisting to push my way through the fallen packets along the side of the wall. At any moment I expect to feel his hands on me again.

He yells, furious. It sounds far enough away that I risk looking over my shoulder.

J is stuck. The gap is too small for him. He can't follow me.

He's knocking packets out of the way, trying to clear a larger passage, but he's too big. His torso barely fits.

I stop and watch him from ten meters away, half hidden behind a large box of machinery.

He notices me looking and stops as well. His mouth, teeth bared in fury as he fights his way to me, transitions into a charming smile.

"Can you help me? I think I'm stuck."

He waves his free hand at me. I slide back another meter, peeking around the corner at him.

"No." The words come out in a whisper.

"No?" he says, feigning confusion.

"I'm not stupid," I tell him. My voice is a little stronger this time.

J stares at me, and then smiles again, flashing white teeth. He wipes away the blood under his nostrils, from where I kicked him.

"I know you're not stupid, Romy. I think you're very clever."

I wince. "Stop lying to me," I say, spitting out the words.

At that, his bright blue eyes actually look surprised. He shifts. The packets around him skid, but he's not trying to chase me anymore. He's settling in to talk.

"Why do you think I'm lying to you?"

"How can you do this to me? I thought we were friends!" I can feel hot tears welling up in the corners of my eyes. I hope he can't see them at this distance.

"What am I doing to you?" he asks, his voice achingly gentle.

"You're . . . you're . . . stalking me. I know you made up the UPR. And the war." My voice is shrill and wavering. I sound like the child he pretends I am.

"You've got it all wrong, Romy. Why don't you come here and I'll explain everything? You can trust me. You know me better than anyone."

I slide back another meter until I can only see the beam from his flashlight and the shadow he casts on the floor as he tries to move. He's quiet, listening to my breathing.

"Nothing you can say will make me trust you. I'd rather die," I whisper, and then slide back, far away from him.

He starts fighting against the packets again. The vibrations make the stacks around me tremble.

He can't get through. There are too many boxes, too densely packed, and I'm too fast. Eventually he gives up.

"I have a heat sensor," he yells. "You can't avoid me forever! Stop acting like a child and come and talk!"

The words stun me. A heat sensor. That's how he found me so quickly. He knew where I was this whole time.

He was toying with me. Again.

I move faster—in case it's a trick, or he's crawling across the stores to cut me off somewhere else. I only stop when my arm hits something that won't shift.

I freeze, wishing I had light. When I check my arm for an

injury, the only fresh blood on me is J's, drying in the cracks of the soles of my feet.

I carefully reach out and touch whatever I hit. It's the rung of a ladder. It's a way out.

I don't bother being quiet—there's no point, not if he can find me so easily. I start climbing downward, even though I don't know where I'm going. I thought I knew every centimeter of my ship, but I can't remember where on the ground level this ladder comes out.

I've been climbing for a few minutes when my stomach twists over and my feet lift out from under me midstep. Suddenly I'm *falling*, colliding with the walls of the shaft on the way down. Something's happened to the artificial gravity.

There's no time to think. I scramble for a rung and twist to the side, trying to catch the ladder, but I'm moving too fast.

I brace myself to hit the floor with a painful and bloody crunch.

Just as I'm really starting to panic, I crash into the base of the shaft, the impact jolting through my knee joints.

I catch my breath, trying to calm my panic. The shaft wasn't deep enough to hurt me. I'm OK.

What's going on? Are the rotation thrusters that control the artificial gravity failing? Or has J done this too? Is he messing with my ship again in an attempt to hurt me?

All he would have to do is adjust the speed at which the ship is rotating. That would change the force of the gravity it generates. To make it heavier, he must have sped up the ship's spinning.

I don't have time to worry about it now. J could push his way through the stores and follow me at any second. I can't let him find me. I start moving, fighting against the force of the new, heavier artificial gravity.

When the shaft's lights flicker off, I don't even stop moving. I pull the flashlight out of my pocket, where I always keep it, and clip it to my belt. My teeth are chattering. It's hard to move, and my limbs are slow to react, like I'm wading through molasses.

I reach down to push open the metal hatch, holding on tightly in case the gravity changes again. The lights flash on and off, strobing across my vision. I feel drunk, unsure which direction is up or down.

I shine my flashlight down into the room below. The dim glow of the blue standby lights turn to white, activated by my motion. Suddenly, I realize where I am. There's a reason I've never come across this ladder before—it leads into the sick bay.

For a second I debate returning to the shaft. I'm caught between finally facing the room or going back to J.

When the lights turn off again and don't come back on, I make my decision. I climb down into the room. Whatever is waiting for me in here is nothing like what's above.

My gaze is drawn to the table where I once found Dad's

remains. The pods still line the room like hollow gravestones. I count from the doorway, finding the one containing my mother.

Now that I'm here, I need to know more than anything: Is she still alive? Or does the pod contain a frozen corpse?

All thoughts of J leave my mind. This is the fear that has consumed me for nearly six years.

I can see the dark shape of my mother's head through the misted glass window. I touch the pod, resting my fingertips where her eyes should be. I hate her for what she did to us. But I also miss her so much it hurts. She's still my mother.

I drop my forehead to the glass, aching to see inside but too scared to look. My other hand touches the side of the pod, wrapping around the machine like I'm hugging her.

To my surprise, it's warm.

I jump back, thinking for a minute that I'm touching human skin, that somehow my mother's hand is dangling out of the pod. Then I realize it's just the warmth of the freezer, working to keep the body inside cool. It's only the machinery, doing its job.

A thought crosses my mind: *warmth.* I cling to it, before fear can drive it away. J's heat sensor. If the pod is warm—if it's giving off heat, like a human—then J won't realize I'm here. He'll think my heat signature is just the pod. I can hide, at least for a while.

If I'm brave enough to stay here, with my mother.

I'm deciding that I don't really have a choice when I notice that there's a brass plaque attached to the front of the pod: *Crew Member: Lucy Shoreditch.*

I trace my fingers over the engraving. Shoreditch. Like . . . J?

I step back and look at the pods on either side. The one on the left says: *Crew Member: Jeremy Shoreditch.*

These must be the names of the astronauts who were in stasis in the pods, back when *The Infinity* was launched.

A man and a woman. With J's surname. Is J short for . . . ?

I'm broken out of my thoughts by the sound of footsteps in the corridor. It's loud, getting closer while I wasn't paying attention—and heading toward the sick bay.

Quickly, I twist behind the pod, squeezing into the confined space between it and the wall. I drop down into a crouch and hope my heat signature blurs with the pod's.

The footsteps stop.

"Romy."

I stop breathing.

"I told you I'd find you."

He won't find me. He won't. He'll see the machine is running and back off. He'll go and look for me somewhere else.

"That was a clever trick with the tunnel. I think I underestimated you."

The footsteps get closer, stopping right in front of the pod. I breathe through my mouth, trying to make as little noise as possible.

There's the *click click click* of fingernails tapping on metal.

I think he's touching the plaque, tracing the words *Lucy Shoreditch*, just like I did.

There's an achingly long silence. Finally, he lets out a huff of laughter.

"Of course you're hiding in here." His voice is bitter. "Where else would you be?" He clears his throat. When he speaks again, the catch in his voice is gone. "I can see you, Romy. Hiding in my mother's tomb."

I know he's not talking about me, only the shadow of the body inside. I still flush hot and then cold with fear. There's a pause, and then, sounding slightly confused, he says, "Can you even hear me in there?"

I catch sight of his hand at the side of the pod, testing the hinge of the lock. There's a beep, and then he pulls open the door of the pod.

"Romy, I—"

His words cut off, and he lets out a little shocked grunt.

I can't help myself—I peer around the side of the pod just in time to watch him tilt backward, the weight of my mother falling onto him.

As she falls, wires tear away from her skin, pinging back into the pod. J staggers, trying to hold her up, but he quickly loses his balance and crashes to the floor. My mother's body lands right on top of him.

J tries to shove her off, but her icy skin has seared to his, like a tongue sticking to an ice cube.

As they roll across the floor, J catches sight of me. He lets out a frustrated yell. "You little—"

He's struggling to get free, to launch himself at me. My mother's forehead is glued to the side of his face. The skin of his cheek pulls and stretches where they touch.

I crawl out from behind the pod and run past him, ignoring his shout of anger. The cold air from the freezer hits me as I pass.

I leave my two nightmares behind me to fight it out between themselves, sprinting down the corridor. I try desperately to *think*. What do I do with my head start? I run as fast as I can, fighting the heavy gravity that J has tried to trap me with.

I've reached the airlock. The place where I first met J; where he entered my ship. I can see *The Eternity* through the closed doors, still connected to *The Infinity*.

Suddenly an idea forms. I can escape. I can take his ship. I can disconnect the two spaceships and just . . . go. Fly off in his ship and leave him here alone in the slower, older one.

He'll never be able to catch up with me, not if I'm in *The Eternity*. It's so fast. He wouldn't be able to get anywhere near me.

When I press the button for the airlock, the doors slide open, one by one. As I step on board *The Eternity*, I feel hope for the first time in longer than I can remember. Hope, and more than that: excitement. I can do this. There's a way out. Suddenly the odds have tipped slightly further in my favor.

I don't give myself time to admire the futuristic design of *The Eternity*, its gleaming metal and mint-green walls. I run down the corridor, scanning the rooms for the helm. I need to detach the ships before J frees himself and works out what I'm doing.

The ship is so huge that I'm not going to be able to find the helm in time by just randomly running around. I stop, gasping for breath.

"Computer?" I say, hoping desperately that there's an audio command system.

A voice immediately comes from the ceiling. *"How can I help you today?"* It's robotic but obviously female: sweet and soft.

I grin around my next sentence, relieved and hysterical. "Can you detach the ship from *The Infinity*, please?"

"Four-letter authorization code required."

I pause. I have no idea. Would J have set the code?

I clear my throat. "Code: Romy?" I wince, hoping that I'm right and wishing to be wrong.

"Access denied. One attempt remaining."

My gut clenches. If I can't guess, then my plan is ruined. I feel sick.

"Is there a way to manually override the code?"

"Authorization code required."

"Code . . ." I waver. The password could be anything at all, just a random string of letters. But I need to try. I need to get away.

I strain my brain, trying to think. Then it occurs to me. J's mother's name. He's mentioned before how much he misses his parents. If anything he told me was true, it might be that. What were the names on the torpor pods? Jeremy Shoreditch. And—

"Code: Lucy?" I say.

There's a pause, and then the computer says, *"Code accepted. Would you like to become the new system administrator?"*

I let out a little sigh of relief, leaning back against the wall.

"Yes, please. Close and secure airlock."

J set his mother's name as the ship's most important password. There was some truth in what he told me—he loved his parents.

"Airlock deactivating. Air pressurization complete," the computer replies after a second.

"Detach the ships, please."

"Ship separation initiated."

I listen, waiting for the sound of the separation. There's nothing for almost a minute, and then a soft shudder rocks the floor.

"No longer in contact with The Infinity. *Shall the ship continue on determined course?"*

My blood pressure drops in seconds. "Yes, as fast as possible."

"Acceleration in progress. Maximum velocity to be obtained."

For almost ten minutes, I stand stock-still, trying to process everything that's happened. I can't believe I'm here. In those long, awful hours in the stores, I gave up all hope of getting away from J. My universe shrank to him and finding a way to escape. Now my universe has expanded again, I don't know what to do with it.

I lick my lips. They are dry and cracked after so long in the stores. I'm warming up, sweating a little. I hadn't even noticed I was cold. But it's hotter on this ship, just slightly. J must have reduced the temperature of *The Infinity* in his effort to force me out of the stores—or to make it easier to track me down with the heat sensor. The gravity is normal here too—not weighing me down when I move.

I shiver, despite the temperature. There's blood on my legs and knuckles. When I touch the tips of my fingers to the wounds, my knees give out beneath me. I need to sit down.

"Computer, where is the helm?"

The voice in the ceiling doesn't speak, but a green line lights up on the floor.

"Thank you!"

I'm quietly amazed. This ship is *so cool*. It makes mine look like it's made out of papier-mâché.

I follow the line around the corner, down another long corridor, and then down another short corridor off that. The ship is huge—at least three times the size of *The Infinity*, based on what I can see so far. There are corridors upon corridors, leading off in every direction. It's so big that I can't believe it's real. It hurts my brain just thinking about it.

Finally, I reach a chrome door that slides open as I approach.

Inside is J's kingdom. The open-plan room is so clearly *his* that it makes me nervous. On one side is a bank of computer screens—that must be the helm. There's also a wide bed against the wall, with sheets tangled up at the foot and pillows punched into balls. The sight of it is the last thing my exhausted brain can process before it gives up completely.

Now that I'm safe, I'm so tired and relieved that I don't even look around. I pass out on J's bed, dropping abruptly into complete unconsciousness.

HOURS SINCE *THE ETERNITY* CAUGHT UP:
38

When I wake up, every muscle in my body aches and I'm desperately thirsty.

I find three half-empty bottles of water and two packets of mac and cheese in a cupboard by the bed. I drink the contents of all three bottles, then eat both packets, crunching through the pasta. I'm starving, but I'm not quite ready to venture out of this room to try and find a proper kitchen.

I'm still wearing my nightie, so I search for clothes. There don't seem to be any in this room, apart from a hoodie that has NASA written on the front in large, stylized letters. I roll up the sleeves of the hoodie and pull it on. It smells like *person*. I'd forgotten that other people have a smell.

Looking around makes me feel like I'm seeing inside J's brain. Dinner packets are strewn on every surface, and there's a tablet on the bed. I open it to find a paused video.

I recognize it as an episode of a TV show he used to talk about. Just like when I found out his password was his mother's name, it catches me by surprise. I hadn't expected any of the things he told me to actually be true. Wasn't he pretending to be Jayden? But this wasn't a lie: he really does watch the show.

Carefully, I click through each tab, seeing what books and essays he's been reading, and what music he last listened to.

It's . . . unnerving. He seems quite normal. He listened to *pop music* yesterday.

Can I really do this? Can I leave him behind? If he stays on *The Infinity*, he'll be in his sixties before he makes it to Earth II, if he ever makes it at all.

Have I condemned J to death?

I don't know what to do. I don't know if I can leave him imprisoned on *The Infinity* like this.

My thoughts are interrupted by a soft, automated voice coming from the tablet. *"There is an incoming call from Jeremy Shoreditch. Would you like to accept?"*

The notification pushes me over the edge.

"Answer it," I say quickly. I need to speak to J. I need to try to understand what's going on.

The video call connects and his face appears.

"Romy," he says.

I can't speak. I just nod, examining his features. I can't tell from his expression whether he's angry or upset. There's a livid red mark on his cheek where my mother's skin had sealed itself to his.

It might just be because I'm safe here on this ship, which is already hundreds of kilometers away from him, but somehow I'm not so terrified anymore. I almost feel sorry for him. Right now, he looks harmless. Exhausted. Not monstrous at all.

When I open my mouth to finally speak, my lips part with an audible sound. "Are you all right?" I ask quietly.

He rubs at the mark on his cheek and sighs. "I'm OK. Romy, I'm sorry I scared you. I should have been more open with you about how soon the ship would be arriving. You're so young, and I . . . I just wasn't thinking coherently."

I bite my lip, fighting back tears. Maybe I should have stopped to talk to him through the airlock, rather than detaching the ships.

"Because of your parents?" I venture carefully. I have barely been able to go anywhere near the sick bay because my mother was in there. If I were him, there's no way I would have been able to deal with boarding the ship my parents died on. Not without some sort of horrifying and embarrassing breakdown.

He nods, then frowns. "I knew it would be hard, coming to the place where they died. But it was so much worse than I thought it would be. The minute I stepped on board, it brought everything back—all the memories of finding out that they'd died, when I felt completely alone in the universe. I got really upset and lashed out at you. I can't tell you how much I regret it."

"I'm so sorry," I whisper. "I didn't know they were part of the crew. I would never have talked about my nightmares in my emails if I'd known that two of the astronauts were your parents."

"I should have told you the truth a long time ago," J says. "But it was just too painful."

"I understand. I can't talk about my . . . about my dad either."

We're both silent.

"How old were you when they died?" I ask. If his parents had him before they left Earth nineteen years ago, then he must have been pretty young.

"Twenty-five. They got accepted for the *Infinity* mission when I was thirteen, which was due to launch after I turned eighteen. At first they weren't sure if they should go, because of me. But NASA told them that I'd be able to follow them in a few years and we'd be together again."

"So when you found out what had happened, you were already trying to become an astronaut too?"

He nods. "I'd just graduated and I was in training at NASA when they told me that Mom and Dad were dead. Just like that. I couldn't believe it. We'd been preparing for so long, and then they were gone before their mission had even really *started*."

"I'm so sorry, J."

He's silent while I wrap my head around everything he's told me.

"They let you join the mission?" I ask. "Even after your parents died in space?"

"Yes. NASA knew I wanted to honor their memory by doing what they couldn't. I had to support what was left of *The Infinity*'s mission. For most of my training we knew that there were still three people alive on the ship—two crew members who hadn't been in stasis when everyone died, and a baby. A little girl. Then, two years before we launched, we found out that an oxygen tank explosion had killed the adults, and the little girl was the only one left. The mission became even more important."

I nod. After they died, I told NASA an oxygen tank had killed my parents. I couldn't bear to explain the truth about my mother. Then I realize what he's saying. "Everyone knew about me?"

J smiles. "Romy, *everyone on Earth* heard about you. The child genius who knows everything there is to know about the ship. Who was going to be the commander when she grew up. I envied you. You had the life that I wanted: exploring the universe with your parents. I started this mission so angry at you for that." J looks down and clears his throat. "You know, I only started talking to you because I wanted to see what you were like. The girl who stole my dream."

I feel raw. This is not what I was expecting to hear.

"That's why I copied your stories," he continues. "I just wanted you to like me. I was trying to get you to open up, to talk to me, so I could see what you were like behind the formal emails you sent as the commander. But now I understand that you'd have talked to me as myself. I didn't need to pretend to be that character."

"It wasn't fair," I say. "It wasn't fair that you manipulated me like that. You used Jayden against me."

"I know. It's the worst thing I've ever done. I regret it so much. Romy, I'm not trying to hurt you. I never will. I swear on it."

"How am I ever supposed to believe that, J? I don't even know what's real anymore. The UPR—are they real or fake? I still don't know!"

"Oh, Romy." J shakes his head. "I'm sorry. The UPR are real. I can see why you would hope they weren't, though. I wish they weren't too."

"But—the coordinates . . ."

He frowns. "All messages from Earth have to be retransmitted to you from *The Eternity*'s transponder, because my ship blocks the path of the signal from there. The messages wouldn't reach you otherwise. Is that what you're talking about?"

I swallow. Why didn't I think of that? "Even if . . . even if the UPR really are in control of our ships, even if their requests are real, there are so many other things that you made up."

"By the end, I wasn't putting on a front anymore, I swear. Those emails were all me. OK, some of the facts about my life were taken from that TV show. I never dropped out of medical school—I've actually got a degree in engineering. And I don't pull pranks on people like Jayden does. But the real stuff—the emotions—that was all me.

"I think after a while, it turned into more than just collecting information. I started to look forward to talking to you. I wasn't expecting us to have so much in common. I showed you more of myself than I ever meant to. We have a genuine bond like I've never felt with anyone before. I fought it for a long time, because I thought I was supposed to hate you, for my parents. But I can't any longer."

I'm silent. I'm too torn up, too impossibly lost, to know how to reply to that.

"I wish things had gone differently," I say into the quiet. "I wish we could have met properly—nicely—without you playing any of these games."

I see his Adam's apple dip as he swallows. "We can still have that. We can start again. Pretend none of this ever happened?"

I hesitate.

I don't trust him. Not at all. How can I? But surely whatever he's done, it's not worth being condemned to this life alone in space. Right?

There's still a part of me that isn't convinced—that remembers how it felt when he grabbed at my knee in the tunnel.

"We don't even have to open the airlock," he adds, looking into the camera with eyes that are full of remorse. "I can stay on *The Infinity* and you can stay on *The Eternity*. We don't ever have to open the door, if you don't want to. Just please don't leave me here."

With that, I'm decided. I wouldn't be able to live with the guilt of abandoning him in space. He can stay on my old ship and I can stay here. We'll travel together, but I'll be safe.

"I'm going to come back and get you," I say.

J smiles, so widely that I can see his perfectly straight teeth. He lifts his arm to run a hand through his golden hair, and that's when I notice the background in the video.

He's standing in front of a wall. A mint-green wall.

Mint. Green.

I know every inch of my ship. There is no mint green anywhere. Not a single centimeter of *The Infinity* is painted mint green.

He's on *The Eternity.*

A shudder rolls down my back. I bite my tongue to stop a gasp. I thought I'd escaped. I thought I was safe. He's on the ship, hiding from me. Pretending he isn't.

He could be anywhere. He could be right behind me.

I force myself not to turn my head and look, even though the hairs on the back of my neck are tingling.

"Oh, Romy," he says, oozing affection. "Thank you so much."

I force my face into a grimacing smile. I nod.

I believed his lies, again. I fell right into another of his traps.

"I thought I'd destroyed everything." He ducks his head and looks up at me through his eyelashes.

"Me too," I say. I can actually feel my heart breaking all over again. He looks so sincere. How is he so good at this? Why is he even doing these things to me? What did I do to deserve *this*?

I force myself to smile again. *Be sweet. Be gentle. Be light.*

"I'll tell the ship to come back for you now," I say, the words coming out brittle, however hard I try. "I'll talk to you soon, OK?"

J nods, and smiles a contented smile. He winks. "See you soon."

I make a weak noise in reply, then disconnect the call. The second his face disappears, I spin around, checking the room.

He's not here.

"Computer, lock the helm door," I say, loud and fast. "Don't allow access to anyone under any circumstances."

"Door locked," the computer confirms.

I'm not convinced. "Will anyone be able to override the lock and get in? Anyone at all?"

"Negative. Access will be restricted to Romy Silvers only."

"Are you absolutely sure?" I can't trust this. Whatever the computer says, J will find a way around it. He's too clever. Too good at programming the software to do what he wants, like with the power malfunctions.

"Only administrators can override a user command."

I speak around clenched teeth. "Are there any administrators on board the ship, right now?"

"Negative."

Finally, I relax from my defensive stance. He can't get in. I'm safe in here, for now.

I'm consumed with self-hatred. I can't believe I was stupid enough to fall for his tricks again. Even knowing what he's like, even after he *chased me across my ship*, I still fell for his lies and charisma—like his taste in books and music would be enough to prove that he's really a good person.

I scrub a hand through my hair and straighten my shoulders. I need to fix my mistakes.

Even if I'm not alone on the ship, I still have an advantage. He can't get in here. I'm safer than I would have been on *The Infinity.*

I'm going to have to leave this room eventually, to get more food and water. This is only a temporary respite, but I have some time to think.

What does he want from me? Is he just torturing me for fun, twisting me around his little finger? Does he like seeing how easily he can persuade me to forgive him?

If I went to him, would he kill me, or would he keep turning good and bad, making me love him and hate him over and over for the sake of it?

I have no idea. I can't understand what he's trying to do. What kind of person thinks like him?

HOURS SINCE *THE ETERNITY* CAUGHT UP:
39

I pace the room, trying to focus despite my panic. When my eyes fall on the helm, a plan of action begins to form. J probably never intended for me to come on board his ship, so anything I find here is the truth. It's not buried beneath layers of lies and manipulation.

I must be able to use that. I can work out who he really is. I can find a weakness somewhere in the hard drive of his ship's computer. He has to have some flaws that I can use against him. It's my only hope.

When the computer wakes up, there's a page open on the screen showing my emails and fanfics. Sentences are highlighted, with comments added in the margins.

It's his notes, his *study of me*.

"You're OK," he said, his voice a low, calming murmur in her ear. "Relax."

She'd never felt so relieved. The tension in her stomach, which had been building in a tight coil since she'd realized she was in danger, dissolved into nothing.

With Jayden, she was safe.

JAYDEN IS CALM IN A CRISIS AND REASSURES LYRA A LOT. NEED TO BE CONFIDENT SO THAT R TRUSTS I KNOW BEST, BUT ALSO CONFESS SOME WEAKNESSES TO MAKE ME SEEM MORE TRUSTWORTHY. CONFIDE EMOTIONALLY IN R TO ACHIEVE THIS.

BRING UP FOOD/COOKING AGAIN—SHE LIKES THAT.

SHE DOESN'T LIKE DISCUSSING HER MOM AT ALL—STICK TO DAD. SOMETHING MUST HAVE HAPPENED WHEN THEY DIED. MAYBE NASA DOESN'T KNOW THE FULL STORY? NOT AN OXYGEN TANK EXPLOSION AT ALL?

Unable to bear it, I minimize the page. There's a new message in his inbox. It's from . . .

Molly.

Just the sight of her name makes me want to cry. I've been so caught up in everything happening with J that I'd completely forgotten to think about her.

Molly. My Molly.

He lied again, then. If Molly is still emailing him, the UPR can't exist. He made them up, just as I suspected.

Even worse, her message is addressed to me. J must have intercepted the signal and blocked it, so it couldn't get to me. Molly never really abandoned me after all.

Trembling, I open the audio message. When Molly's gentle voice starts speaking—so familiar even after all this time—I let out a sob. I can't stop the tears that fall long after the message has finished playing.

From: NASA Earth   Sent: 03/05/2066
To: The Infinity   Received: 12/05/2067
Attachment: EarthII-sim.zip [8 GB]

Audio transcript: Hi, Romy, I hope you're having a good day! It snowed here yesterday, and Nino is having such fun discovering snowflakes for the first time. He keeps trying to eat them!

I'm attaching an updated version of the Earth II simulation, which will let you practice the landing protocols for the larger combined vessel of *The Eternity* and *The Infinity*. It also includes better graphics, and training exercises for some of the new pieces of agricultural equipment.

I've been testing it for you, and it's really fun—I think you'll enjoy it! I'm jealous that you get to play the whole thing.

Talk to you tomorrow, sweetie.

My heart hurts.

Molly has been sending me audio messages all this time. There are hundreds of messages, one for every single day since *The Eternity* launched and J started blocking them from reaching me. It feels like a punch in the gut.

Molly has no idea what J has been doing to me for the last

year. She doesn't know about any of the ways he's been tormenting and torturing me. She thinks I'm perfectly happy.

I scroll through the pages of messages from Molly in the inbox, addressed to both J and me. Then I check the sent emails, to find out what J has been saying to NASA in reply.

From: The Eternity   Sent: 12/05/2067
To: NASA Earth   Predicted date of receipt: 09/15/2069

Dear Dr. Molly Simmons,

We are afraid to report that the laser transmitter on *The Infinity* is still broken. Below is Commander Silvers's latest message to NASA Earth, as received on *The Eternity* via *The Infinity*'s short-distance radio transmitter.

We are working with Commander Silvers to advise her on the best method of fixing the long-distance laser transmitter, and seem to be making good progress. Hopefully the problem will soon be fixed and she will be able to return to regular communication methods.

Hoping all is well on Earth,

Commander Shoreditch and Pilot Evans

Attached message reads:

From: The Infinity   Sent: 12/05/2067
To: NASA Earth   Predicted date of receipt: 09/15/2069

Hi, Molly!

I wish I could play in the snow with Nino. That sounds so cool!

Thank you for the software. I've already tested it and it's brilliant.

Jeremy, Isaac, and I are working hard to fix the transmitter here on *The Infinity*. I really hope we get it working soon—I miss talking to you properly!

Love, Romy

It sounds just like me. For months and months, J has been telling Molly lie after lie, pretending to be me. And who is *Isaac*—is he "Pilot Evans"? I've never heard J mention another person being on board *The Eternity*, but "pilot" implies there is a second in command. The ship must have launched with *two* crew members. So where is Isaac Evans now?

Has . . . has J done something to him?

Oh God. I hope Isaac is OK.

I make myself listen to more of Molly's messages. The sound of her voice is like a hug, even with the obvious concern and worry in everything she says. I've missed her so much.

I wish I could email Molly and ask for help. I wish there was a way she could save me and make J go away forever. But there isn't. I'm on my own.

I close down the emails. I'm not going to find anything else useful there, just bad memories.

I run my shaking hands through my hair and let out a

frustrated yell. I deserve so much better than this. I deserve so much better than him. He destroys everything he touches, but I can't—let—him—destroy—me.

I'd do anything to find a way to lock him up. I would push him into a stasis pod without a moment's hesitation, just so I never had to think about him again. I wouldn't even feel guilty about it.

I start looking through his drawers, searching for anything I can use as a weapon. I need a way to defend myself while I work out how to end this.

If I can just get him back to *The Infinity* and trap him in a pod, this will all go away. He wouldn't even see it coming. Not from needy, gullible Romy, desperate for affection. Not from the little mouse caught between his claws.

I know it's a desperate plan, with barely a chance of success, but I need to try.

I find a pair of scissors in the desk and test the blade against the pad of my thumb. When I press it into the skin, it leaves a white line behind. It's not sharp, but if I use enough force, it might work. Either way, it's going to have to do. If I press it against his back, he won't be able to tell the difference between scissors and a knife.

When I've searched the whole room and failed to find anything else that could be useful, I go over to the computer and say, "Locate Jeremy Shoreditch."

I need to do this now, before I start second-guessing

myself. Before he has the chance to persuade me to trust him again.

A map appears on the screen, with a glowing orange symbol showing J's location. He's just down the corridor from the helm. It looks like he's waiting to ambush me. He must have found the door locked and decided to wait for me to come out. I can't even imagine how he plans for all of this to end.

I wonder if he would admit that he's right outside the room if I called him now. Not that I care. Whatever he says, I'm not going to listen.

I prepare myself, wrapping my fist around the scissors and putting a blank expression on my face. I take a deep breath, telling myself that I'm strong and brave and I can handle this. I have no other choice.

"Open the door."

As soon as it begins to open, I start running.

J is standing in the center of the hallway waiting for me. I sprint at him, fist clenched around the pair of scissors, out of sight behind my back.

"Romy!" he says, feigning surprise, but that's as far as he gets before I run straight at him. I'm picturing driving the blade into the flesh of his stomach when he grabs me by the arms and lifts me up, pushing me back against the wall. I flail and kick, dropping the scissors as I try to get free. He holds me in midair like I weigh nothing, and knocks back my blows without even trying.

"Let go!" I shout, horrified that he managed to stop me so easily.

"Don't even try," he growls. "You're coming with me."

He roughly twists my wrists behind my back, holding them with one hand even as I struggle to break free. He wraps his other arm around my throat from behind.

"If you fight, I'll break your neck," he whispers into my ear.

I immediately go still, waiting to see what he's going to do next. I bare my teeth but don't risk replying.

He takes a step forward, forcing me to march in front of him, away from the scissors, which are lying on the floor.

We walk down three corridors, turning right and left and right again. I rack my brain for some way I can get free, and what else I could use as a weapon, but I'm so frightened that my mind has gone completely blank. It's all I can do to take step after step.

Finally, J stops outside a door, his arm tightening on my throat like he's pulling on a horse's reins.

The door slides open. I see a hospital bed in the middle of the room and realize he's brought me to this ship's sick bay. I wonder if this is where he brought Isaac. Is he going to kill me the same way he must have killed him?

The bed is hooked up to an IV. I'm imagining what he's going to do to me—if he's going to cut me up or knock me out cold, or worse—when I notice that . . . there's someone in the bed, chest rising and falling in the steady rhythm of sleep.

J pushes me toward them.

It's my mother. She's not in stasis anymore. She's *alive*.

After all this time, she's still alive.

HOURS SINCE *THE ETERNITY* CAUGHT UP:
40

When I see my mother, I start struggling in J's grip.

"No! NO! *NO!*" I scream. "Stop!"

"Shh," J murmurs. "You don't want to wake her up, do you?"

I stop fighting. No. I don't want that. Not in a million years.

J loosens his arm, but pulls me in closer so that my back is pressed up against his front.

My mother is alive. I can't deal with this. I want desperately to disappear inside my head like she used to, so I don't have to process what's happening, but I can't.

"What are you doing?" I say in a desperate, quiet voice. "She's dangerous! She killed my dad!"

He snorts. "She can barely move. She's been in stasis—she's got reduced muscle strength. How is your mother still alive, by the way?" he asks, curious and calm. "You told NASA that both of your parents died in an oxygen tank explosion almost six years ago."

"I lied," I gasp. I can't let him wake her up. I need to keep him talking, to distract him. "I couldn't tell NASA the truth about what she did."

He hisses through his teeth. "I had everything planned out so neatly, thinking you were alone. This has changed everything. But I can work with it. I can't believe that after everything she did, she's *still alive*."

"Please don't. Whatever you're doing, stop. I thought we had a connection," I add, half to delay him by talking, half because I still don't understand, not even a little bit. "I thought you *liked me*."

"I do like you," he says, confused. Once again, he sounds genuine. How did he get so good at lying? "You're sweet, Romy."

"Then why are you doing this?" I say.

"Why don't we ask your mother to explain?"

"No!" I cry, but it's too late. He's already shouting.

"GOOD MORNING, TALIA!"

Time freezes around us for a second. Then my mother stirs, half opening her eyes. She looks woozy.

"Over here!" he trills to her. My mother blinks, her gaze wandering the room until she spots us. Her expression sharpens from hazy to awake in seconds.

Without warning, I throw up, chunks of mac and cheese

forcing their way past J's arm on my throat, spraying down the front of my top and onto the floor.

J makes a disgusted noise in my ear and moves away from me, leaving a space between our bodies. "Jesus Christ."

I draw in a deep gasp of air, trying not to choke.

"You should never have woken her up!" I tell him, spitting bile onto the floor.

He doesn't know what happened to Dad. He has no idea what she's capable of.

My mother is wide awake now. She's watching us carefully. She coughs quietly, testing her throat.

"Don't worry," J says into my ear. "I'll look after you."

The words echo what J always said in my daydreams, when we first met and fell in love. I fight back another wave of vomit. The fiction I created about us feels like the naive nonsense of a child.

"Please," I gasp. "Whatever you're planning, you can't— Don't—"

"Romy?" The words, uncertain and hoarse, come from my mother. I stop talking abruptly.

"Mum?" I say. The sound of her voice makes me feel like I'm eleven again.

"Romy, who is that man?" Her words are calm—nothing like the manic shriek I remember from when I last saw her, smashing up the embryos.

"Mum!" I choke back a sob.

I used to crave the days when she was lucid more than anything else in the world. Even now, I want to run to her, to hide under her arm and breathe in her smell, despite the image that never leaves my mind: her pushing Dad away, him falling onto broken glass.

"Mum, you have to help me!" I say, desperately grasping at a fragile hope. "He's going to kill me!"

"I'm going to kill you both, actually." J jerks his arm against my neck, casually testing his strength. It's a reminder of how powerless I am.

"Let go of her," my mother says, struggling to sit up in bed. "You're hurting her!"

"Oh, Talia. I'm going to do much more than *hurt* your daughter. I'm going to make you sit and watch as I kill her," J says. "And then I'm going to kill you."

Tears stream down my face. "Why are you doing this?" I wail.

"Haven't you worked it out yet?" he spits. "This is my *revenge*. Your parents killed my mom and dad. Dr. Silvers here was too busy fawning over her perfect little newborn baby to actually *do her fucking job*."

Suddenly, everything makes sense. "That wasn't their fault!" His parents' deaths were just an accident. He's so lost in grief that he can't see the truth.

He laughs. "Not their fault? You have nightmares about the astronauts *every single night*, Romy. Why are you so frightened of them? What possible reason could you have to be so scared of long-dead crew members?"

I don't understand what point he's making. Anyone would fear the astronauts, wouldn't they? "They're . . . It's scary! The thought of them, it's—"

He shakes his head, talking over me. "You're guilty. You know that if you hadn't been born, the astronauts would still be alive."

"No, you're wrong!" I deny it, but my mind is racing. Is that really the reason? Have I really felt like their deaths were my fault, all these years? Hundreds of lives, lost. Because . . . of me?

"The torpor technology failed," I say, weak and uncertain now in the face of his conviction. "There was nothing that could have saved them. Even if I hadn't been born, they would still have died."

He squeezes his hand tight around both of my wrists. I hear the bones creak, and pain shoots up my arms.

"You know that's not true. Your parents were supposed to wake up my mom and dad five years into the journey. They were going to take over as caretakers while your parents went into stasis. But then you were born, so they stayed awake to raise little baby Romy. And my parents *died*. Along with hundreds of other astronauts!"

But any mother would choose their baby over stasis, however important the mission was. NASA had even told them to stay awake. "But—"

He doesn't let me speak. "If Talia hadn't been so selfish, then my parents would be alive right now. They might even have noticed the failure in the stasis pods and woken everyone up before it was too late. Instead, *everyone* is dead."

"It's not my mother's fault she got pregnant," I say, refusing to accept that he's right. I know that my mother felt guilty about the astronauts, but I never really believed that she was responsible. How could she be? "Accidents happen. You can't blame all of this on a mistake!"

"She didn't just accidentally get pregnant. She must have removed her birth control—all female crew members were fitted with IUD coils. It was intentional. She knew what a risk it would be to the mission, and she did it anyway. She destroyed *everything*. For you."

When I turn to her, I can see from her expression that J is right. I was never a "happy accident."

Suddenly, so much of my childhood makes sense. This really is her fault. She knew that. The reason she couldn't look at me, for years after the astronauts died, was because she felt guilty.

My brain stops fighting to deny this. J is right. My mother chose to have a baby, and because of that, she held herself responsible for the deaths of hundreds of astronauts.

But that isn't enough to explain everything he has done to me.

"Even if it is her fault, why did you make up all those lies to *me*?" I say, salty tears dripping into my mouth. "Why the games? Why did you invent the UPR? If all you want is revenge, why not just kill me when you arrived? Why torture me for months like that?"

"I was telling the truth when I said I was curious about you. That's how it started. Then I realized that I had the perfect opportunity to make you suffer. To make you feel the pain I felt when my mom and dad died."

Even though he said we had a connection, he never actually identified with me at all. He just saw his need for revenge. Nothing I've ever said, and nothing I can say now, is going to change his mind. This will end in one of two ways—he kills me, or I kill him.

I bite down on the inside of my cheek, forcing myself to be calm.

"Your parents wouldn't want you to do this," I say, stalling for time. "Think of Lucy. And . . . and Jeremy."

Without warning, he twists my wrists in his grip until I hear a snap. I cry out, unable to think about anything but the pain in my left arm, searing hot and impossibly brutal.

"How *dare you*. You don't know a single thing about my parents."

"But *I* do," my mother says, her voice hard. "They were good people. They wouldn't have wanted this."

"I don't believe a fucking word you say," J hisses.

"Lucy was one of my closest friends," my mother continues. "Jeremy and I were partners for most of our in-class training.

Do you think I didn't mourn them? Do you really think it didn't destroy me, inside and out, to have to admit that I'd lost them? Whatever you do to me, Jeremy, trust me, it can't be worse than what I've done to myself."

"I don't care how sad you are," J says. "Your bleeding heart isn't going to bring them back. I met you, before the ship launched. Do you even remember? A month before take-off, at a dinner party for the family of the crew. They'd just announced that you and your husband would be the first set of caretakers. After dessert was served, you *promised* me you'd take care of my parents while they were in stasis. You looked me dead in the eye and said that to my face."

"I remember, Jeremy," she says. I can do nothing but look between them, fighting the pain shooting up my arm long enough to focus on what's happening.

"I told you that I'd been accepted on an astrophysical engineering course. That I wanted to be an astronaut, to join the colony on Earth II one day," J continues. He twists his head to the side and wipes away tears on his shoulder. "You said that you'd make sure my mom and dad were waiting for me."

"I did," my mother says, quiet, agonized.

"It was all a lie!" he shouts.

"Let her go, Jeremy," my mother repeats. She's still struggling to sit up, her arms trembling with the effort. "I admit it. I'm a terrible person. I've spent years hating myself for what I did. But *please* leave Romy out of this. She was only a little girl.

This isn't her fault. She's a good person—the best. If you've been talking to her, you must know that."

"Of course I know that," J yells. He's breathing in short bursts, hot against my cheek. "But why should she get to live? Why should she get to be happy? If she didn't exist, *my parents would still be alive!*"

J's hands are still squeezing around my broken wrist, so tight the pain makes my vision go black.

My mother lets out a feeble, furious yowling sound, like a dying cat desperately trying to protect her kitten. She jerks out of the bed on wobbly legs, stumbling toward us with her arm raised.

Through the spots in my vision I can see something in her hand, something sharp and metallic.

It's a hypodermic syringe, filled with some kind of liquid.

She dives for J, who pushes me away so that I stumble and nearly fall over. I catch myself on the end of the bed, my weight landing on my broken wrist and making me dizzy.

By the time I steady myself enough to turn around, J has caught my mother's arm. They wrestle, but my mother is still weak from the stasis. It's only the threat of the syringe that keeps him from overpowering her immediately.

I tear my eyes away from them. This might be my only chance to find another weapon, something better than the scissors I dropped in the corridor. I need to look now, while J is distracted with my mother. Maybe I can save us both.

I run over to the surgical counter and start pulling open drawers, scattering bandages and pill packets across the floor as I search for something—anything—sharp enough to hurt. Sharp enough to kill.

A series of thuds sounds from behind me. I spin, just in time to watch J overpower my mother. He pushes her hand down and jabs the needle of the syringe into her thigh.

She lets out a horrified cry when he presses down on the plunger, but carries on fighting him. The syringe empties into her flesh, crimson blood filling up the chamber.

Heat flushes through me. It's too late. He'll come for me next, and I've found nothing I can use to defend myself.

Running across the room, I yank at the handle of a door, ignoring the sound of fighting behind me.

As soon as I slam shut the door, I press the keypad on the wall. The lock slides into place with a neat click.

Breath leaves me in a rush. I've bought myself a tiny bit of time. I'm in a supply cupboard—there must be something in here that I can use. Some kind of surgical equipment would work.

I start rifling through boxes on the shelves, but I keep thinking about my mother's blood clouding the syringe. I wonder what was injected into her. It must be something dangerous, if she was planning to use it as a weapon.

I shake myself. I need to keep looking. The only way to help her now is to stop him.

I sift through more bandages, tweezers, towels. Nothing useful. Nothing dangerous.

There's a rattling at the door handle. Spinning around, I watch it move up and down, then fall still. Lights flash on the keypad. He's trying to get in.

Diving across the room, I press buttons, trying to counter his orders. The door unlocks, and then locks again.

This is the same system used for the doors on *The Infinity*. If I can take the front panel off the keypad, then I think I can cut the wires and break the lock so that J can't open it at all. It happened once to the bathroom door on *The Infinity*. The wiring failed and it froze shut. We had to take the door off its hinges.

I grab a plastic bottle off the shelves and use it to smash the keypad, throwing all my weight into each swing until the plastic panel shatters into pieces. J's beeping pauses, and then restarts faster.

I pull at the panel until there's enough space to reach behind. I run my fingers over the wires, searching for the one I know will break the lock. I tear the wire free, pulling my hand away just as the circuit board sparks with electricity.

The screen goes dark. It worked.

The door shudders. He must be hitting it. He's going to break it down.

The handle starts jerking, like he's trying to work it free. A memory flashes across my mind: my mother, replacing a circuit board. Saying to me, "Don't touch the wires, Romy. They'll shock you."

I pick up the loose wire, still sparking with electricity, and press it to the metal door handle. A white flash blinds me as power jumps between them.

There's a hoarse, pained noise. The handle stops moving. I hear a muffled thud as J falls to the floor.

The fuse must have shorted, because the soft ceiling lighting fades into black. I press my ear to the door, but I can't hear anything.

The electricity could have been enough to kill him. I hope.

My breathing sounds wet and loud in the silence. I still need a weapon, just in case he's alive. I need to be prepared.

I start searching through boxes by touch, carefully turning over items until I know what they are, until I'm certain they aren't useful.

The lights come back on while I'm looking through the final shelf, illuminating a box labeled "Scalpels." I open it with stiff, numb fingers, pulling out a sharp knife. This time, I don't even need to test the blade.

When the shining metal catches the light, I realize I'm trembling. I brace my muscles, trying to stop it. I need a strong, firm grip.

There's still no noise from the next room. I can't even hear my mother.

I want to stay in here, safe and alone, but if there's a chance she's still alive then I need to help her. I can't hide again like last time.

I pull the emergency release lever at the top of the door. It slides open halfway, shudders, then stops in its tracks.

J is lying on the floor. He's pale, and his left arm is covered in dark burns from where he must have been holding the door handle when he was electrocuted. His breathing is shallow but even.

He's still alive.

I turn sideways and squeeze through the gap between the door and the doorjamb. The air smells of burnt meat, sharp and acrid.

J groans and rolls toward me.

"Romy." His voice is hoarse.

I don't hesitate. I bend down and thrust the scalpel up into the side of his stomach. It's so tough that for a moment I think I've hit his belt, until I feel the tacky warmth of blood in between my fingers. His face, still slack from unconsciousness, twists in pain.

My eyes fill with tears, but I blink them away and twist the blade, driving it as far into his guts as I can reach. The impact vibrates down my arm as it hits something dense.

J reaches up, hands sliding across my elbows, both of us slippery with blood. I pull free, driving the knife into his chest.

Air explodes from his lungs in a thick, watery cough, and his hand comes up, fist pushing into the wound, trying to quench the blood. He drops his head back, making a sound that's half groan, half frustrated laugh.

"I always told you that you were stronger than you realized, didn't I, Romy Silvers?"

I stare down at him, my vision buzzing with spots of black. I can't think of anything worth saying to him. Instead, I turn to my mother. She's collapsed on the end of the hospital bed, looking down at the needle sticking out of her thigh. As soon as I read the resignation in her expression, I know it's hopeless.

I pull out the needle and read the label on the syringe. It's a lethal injection.

She sacrificed herself to protect me?

"I'm sorry, Romy," she says.

"It's not your fault. You . . . you tried your best. And I got him. He's dying."

She gasps, grimacing in pain. "That's not what I meant."

I know what she means. J is a tiny droplet in the ocean of issues between us.

"Why did you do it?" I whisper. "How could you just let Dad die like that, without even trying to save him? You just *stood there*."

She opens her mouth to answer, but her eyes are already drifting shut. My mind replays the moment of his death, the look in her eyes when Dad fell into that smashed freezer door. But now I don't see anger and murderous rage. I see pain, and fear, and helplessness. She was lost, and in agony.

Sobs rack my body. "You left me alone. You left me all on my own."

I thought it was *me*. I thought she hated me so much that she couldn't look at me, that she would rather die in stasis than be alone with me. But she wanted a child so desperately that she removed her birth control. She ignored NASA's rules.

I was wanted. I was really, truly *wanted*.

She loved me so much, so deeply. That just wasn't enough to stop the pain when her friends died because of that love.

"I didn't want to hurt you," she whispers. She looks so small and fragile. Nothing like the terrible version of her that exists in my memory.

She saved me. She left me alone so that she wouldn't hurt me too.

I reach out to touch her neck, fingers pressed against her pulse. J lets out a long groan behind me, but I ignore him. He's too injured to move, let alone find another way to hurt me.

There is nothing to fear here—just a sad woman who has been in pain for a long time. She would never hurt me intentionally. She never meant to hurt Dad.

"I forgive you," I say finally, not sure it's true yet, but knowing that one day it will be—and I need her to hear it, in her final moments.

Her mouth forms the word "sorry," but she's unconscious before she can make a sound.

It takes a long time for her heart to still. By the time her eyes have stopped darting back and forth beneath her lids, the tears have dried on my cheeks.

My mother is gone, at last. I wish things had been different. But part of me is glad that I got to say good-bye, instead of leaving her in stasis for the rest of my life, caught somewhere between life and death. Neither of us able to move on.

I stand up. My whole body screams in pain.

At some point while I was holding my mother, J went still and silent. He looks so small now, so underwhelming. When I touch my foot to his shoulder, he doesn't react. He's dead.

J is dead. My mother is dead. I'm alive.

It was the only way this could have ended.

HOURS SINCE *THE ETERNITY* CAUGHT UP:
41

I leave my mother and J lying in the sick bay and stagger out of the room, dropping onto my hands and knees in the corridor. My chest feels tight, and every time I breathe I think I'm about to start crying again, but the tears won't come.

I'm in shock. I'm not having a heart attack, or a stroke, or dying. I'm just in shock.

I curl up on the floor, staring at the mint-green wall and shuddering, reliving the last few hours over and over. *The dense sponginess of J's stomach when I pushed the knife inside him. The smell of burnt flesh after he was electrocuted. The feeling of him dragging me down the corridor, squeezing my wrists. The utter, heart-stopping fear when I realized that he was on* The Eternity *with me.*

I can't focus on anything. Half-formed thoughts flicker through my mind, appearing and disappearing before I can process them.

I want to go back into the sick bay, to make sure J is really dead. I want to push his body out of the airlock so that he can never follow me again. I want to tear my brain out of my skull, so I never remember what happened, so I can get rid of this awful, aching feeling.

Finally, the only thing that gets me moving is the realization that I'm cold. My teeth are chattering. Shivering, clammy with sweat, I crawl down the corridor, searching for something. I'm not sure what.

A door on my left slides open when I approach, and I go inside. It's a bathroom. I pull every towel out of the cupboard, wrapping them around me, layer after layer absorbing slick blood and salty sweat.

What do I do now? What is next?

They're gone. They're both gone.

I want my own bunk. I want to be back on my ship, in the rooms I know—not this alien, *mint-green* thing the size of a planet.

I walk out of the bathroom, moving down another corridor, taking myself farther away from the sick bay.

The thud of my heartbeat in my ears when J tried to unlock the supply cupboard door. His breath, hot against my neck when he hissed into my ear. The shock wave of horror when he appeared in the stores, staring at me through the crack between packets.

I walk, following lines of red and blue that light up in the floor.

What do I do?

I find a habitation area and sit on a sofa, still wrapped in a thick swath of blood-soaked towels.

J's emails. J's awful, wonderful emails. I shudder, swallowing against the sour taste at the back of my mouth.

The audio calls. Hearing him breathe, waiting for me to speak. His silhouette, standing in the doorway of the airlock when the ships connected. Standing and waiting for me to arrive and see him there.

I tip over and, without quite realizing it, pass out.

HOURS SINCE *THE ETERNITY* CAUGHT UP:
63

When I wake up, my eyes won't open. I rub at layers of sleep gunk and salt from crying, but my eyelashes still hurt when I force them open.

J. My mother. The sick bay. Wires. Scalpel.

I feel so dirty. There's blood all over me, scabbing and crisp and peeling. I long for my own ship, my own bed, my own life. My den to hide in. But I'm stuck here, at least for now.

I walk to the bathroom, leaving a cocoon of towels on the sofa. There's a shallow ringing in my ears. My mouth is so dry I'm not sure I could talk. When I open my lips, flakes of red blood fall to the floor. I wonder vaguely if it's mine.

My left wrist is throbbing. I cradle it against my chest as I sift through drawers for a first-aid kit. I tie it up, and then run a bath. When I rinse the last few days off my skin, it turns the water a pale brown.

Whenever I jar my wrist, J's actions flash through my mind again. I push them away, focusing on just cleaning myself. One step at a time. Once I'm clean, then I can decide what to do next. Then I can think about all the things I need to do: get back in touch with Molly; learn how to operate this ship; wait for *The Infinity* to catch up; get rid of the bodies. But for now, all I need to do is clean myself. Brush my hair. Find some clothes. Eat.

One step at a time. Slow and easy. Nothing scary. Nothing to fill me with horror, or freeze me with indecision.

I close my eyes, tipping my head back and letting the water fill my ears until the low throbbing of the ship's rotation disappears into a heavy silence.

Nice and simple.

HOURS SINCE *THE ETERNITY* CAUGHT UP:
135

Three days later, I finally feel like I can breathe again. I've spent most of that time in bed watching TV. Not *Loch & Ness*—not yet. There are too many reminders of J in everything Jayden says. I watch films instead, every Christmas and holiday romance I can find on *The Eternity*'s hard drive.

I can't stop watching. Whenever I go to the kitchen or bathroom, or try to sleep, or even just look away from the screen, J's face flashes through my mind.

I know I'm going to have to face the memories eventually. I've been through this before, when Dad died. Molly used to tell me that I couldn't just pretend it hadn't happened. That I had to work through my feelings and accept them.

But I'm not ready. Not yet.

The only comfort is that I'm not frightened of my mother anymore. The thought of Mum just makes me feel achingly, tearfully sad. Which, I think, is an odd kind of progress.

I finally understand her, for the first time in years. I know why she did the things she did. I know why she found it so hard to spend time with me after the deaths of the crew. I don't blame her. I even miss her now.

She was trying to deal with the bad decisions she'd made in the best way she knew how. She never meant to hurt any of us. She was just too weak, too lost, too guilty.

Everything I am, I get from my parents. I would never have survived J—survived life alone on *The Infinity*—if it wasn't for the skills they have given me. My mother taught me about emergency protocols, first aid and ship maintenance. I wouldn't have known how to detach the wires in the door to escape J if it hadn't been for her advice all those years ago. She saved my life.

I've done some horrifying things; things I never thought I was capable of. But it was right. I don't doubt that. It could have been a lot worse. For once, I did what I needed to do. I didn't panic. I didn't cry. I just did it.

When I run out of romcoms and my legs start to spasm from lying in one position for too long, I begin to explore the ship. At first, I check around every corner. Some part of my brain is still convinced that J is lying in wait, ready to pounce. But as I cover more ground, I start to relax.

I'm alone. He's gone, forever. I defended myself, and I never need to be scared of him again.

When I open the door of a room near the sick bay, it takes me a long time to process what's inside. Pods. Hundreds of them. Stasis chambers stretch as far as I can see.

As soon as I realize what it means—that the new ship is full of sleeping people, and they are grown-ups, not just embryos—I burst into tears.

I hadn't imagined there would be any stasis pods on this ship, not after the astronauts died last time. But NASA must have fixed the technology. All this time, J was just the care-taker who stayed awake for the journey. He wasn't the main passenger.

When I read the name *Isaac Evans* on the front of one of the pods, my tears increase with relief. J didn't kill him, like I suspected. There's someone inside, so he must have forced him into stasis so he could get me alone.

I walk the aisles, running my hands across the pods. NASA has sent me a whole colony. There are hundreds of people, right here. I'm never going to be alone again.

I wipe away my tears, and press the *revive* button on the nearest pod.

HAPPILY EVER AFTER

by TheLoneliestGirl

Fandom: Loch & Ness (2042)

Relationship: Gen

Tags: Space AU

Summary: Lyra is finally at peace.

Author's note:

Hi, Earth (Hi, Molly!),

It's been a long time. A lot has happened recently, but I'm not quite sure how to put it into words.

The ships have met and joined together now. *The Eternity* did have to slow down for a while and wait for *The Infinity* to catch up, but we recovered the speed. Our estimated arrival date on Earth II is now November 2071. I'll be twenty.

For once, I'm not scared. I can't wait. I'm not sure what it will be like on Earth II, or what problems we might have to deal with during the rest of our journey. But whatever happens, I think I can handle it.

Molly, I can't say that I've become the confident, brave woman you hoped I would, but I think I'm getting there. I think I'm going to be OK, Molly. I really do.

Love, Romy

Lyra wiped sweat off her forehead, peering up into the pink sky. She stretched out her back, which ached after a morning spent planting seedlings.

The three moons gleamed brightly overhead, crossing the sky in a not-quite-straight line. Only a few more minutes until they aligned, she decided.

She pulled out her water bottle and drank deeply, eyes following *The Infinite Eternity* as it landed in a cloud of luminescent dust, bringing in a cargo of minerals to the colony from the next planet over.

"Happy anniversary!" a little girl said as she ran down the lane.

Lyra smiled after her, watching an excitable puppy jump around at the girl's ankles. When she looked back up at the sky, the moons had made a perfect stripe across the horizon.

"Five years today," Lyra murmured, hardly able to believe it. "Doesn't time fly?"

fin.

ACKNOWLEDGEMENTS

Thank you to my agent, Claire Wilson, and my editors, Emily McDonnell, Emilia Rhodes, and Annalie Grainger. You've been the dream team. Thanks to everyone at Walker Books, Rogers, Coleridge & White, and HarperCollins US, especially Rosie Price, Rosi Crawley, Katarina Jovanovic, Gill Evans, Sorrel Packham, Claudia Medin, Maria Soler Cantón, and Iree Pugh.

This novel was supported by an Arts Council England grant.

Thank you to the Ogden Trust for inviting me on a physics symposium during Lower Sixth, where I learned about special relativity and struggled over a time dilation calculation which inspired this novel. You can read a similar question on pages 50–51.

As usual, thank you to my family and friends. Especially Chris for being a sounding board while I calculated transmission dates on my ridiculous Excel spreadsheet, Sarah for #SaveRomySilvers, Alice for the late-night guidance counselling, and Mum for the tireless proofreading.

This is a work of fiction. As such, some of the more complex aspects of space travel have been simplified for the sake of the narrative.